Tacey Cromwell

Tacey Cromwell

Conrad Richter

Introduction by William T. Pilkington

A Zia Book

UNIVERSITY OF NEW MEXICO PRESS

Albuquerque

*The characters and situations in this work
are wholly fictional and imaginary, and do
not portray and are not intended to portray
any actual persons or parties.*

Copyright 1942 by Conrad Richter. Copyright renewed 1970 by
Harvena Richter. All rights reserved. University of New Mexico
Press paperback edition reprinted 1974 by arrangement with
Harvena Richter and Paul R. Reynolds, Inc.
Introduction copyright 1974 by the University of New Mexico
Press.
Manufactured in the United States of America.
Library of Congress Catalog Card Number 74-84234
International Standard Book Number 0-8263-0361-7

INTRODUCTION

Tacey Cromwell is a representative sample of Conrad Richter's fiction. Composed in the author's graceful and polished prose, the novel reads, as do all his books, smoothly and rapidly. Thematically Tacey Cromwell typifies Richter's lifelong interest— an interest manifested in a number of his works— in the processes of human growth and development, in the factors that influence and mold an individual's personality. Its narrative point of view is also characteristic of the writer's fiction, and that point of view—the reminiscence of a mature man remembering his youth—inevitably bathes the tale in nostalgia; it is not, however, an offensively sentimental nostalgia. In fact, in this one area at least the novel is, to my taste, superior to The Sea of Grass, since its elegiac tone is more expertly handled and better controlled than that of the latter book.

Conrad Richter was born in Pine Grove, Pennsylvania, in 1890, and at the time of his death in 1968 he had come full circle and was once again living in Pine Grove. But the place of residence most potent in stimulating his literary gifts was not his native village; it was instead Albuquerque, where he made his home for more than two decades—from 1928 to 1950. In New Mexico, Richter was fascinated by the rugged landscape and, more important to his writing, by the lore and legendry of the Southwest. Over the years he meticulously culled newspapers and other printed sources bearing on the region's history, and he interviewed scores of oldtimers whose tales and firsthand information on the settling and taming of the Southwest provided valuable background material for several of his fictions. Richter wrote about the East of his early years in ten novels and five times as many short stories—most notably in *The Trees* (1940), *The Fields* (1946), and *The Town* (1950), his trilogy of the Ohio frontier. But the arid land of the American Southwest and its colorful history proved the more forceful inspiration, prompting the writer's best and most creative work.

Richter's southwestern fiction consists of a handful of short stories, collected in *Early Americana* (1936), and three novels: *The Sea of Grass* (1937), *Tacey Cromwell* (1942), and *The Lady* (1957). The best of the novels is unquestionably *The Sea of Grass*, a work generally recognized as one of the classics of western American literature. On a level of achievement slightly lower than that of the author's masterpiece, I believe, are *Tacey Cromwell* and *The Lady*. But however one ranks the novels in terms of quality, a reading of any one of them serves as a useful introduction to Richter's southwestern books, since all three feature similar themes and methods of development.

The three novels, for example, may be loosely

categorized in a genre very common to American
fiction—the initiation story, in which the main character passes from youthful innocence to knowledge
and maturity. Like the narrators of *The Sea of
Grass* and *The Lady*, "Nugget" Oldaker, the narrator of *Tacey Cromwell*, is a middle-aged man
whose reminiscences recall the exciting events and
personalities that, for him, were the bridge between
childhood and adulthood. The perspective afforded
by this point of view creates a gently ironic effect, as
the reader contrasts the worldly wisdom of the older
narrator with the naïveté of the inexperienced boy
who is a participant in the plot. Unfortunately the
point of view also causes technical problems in that
Nugget, especially in the last half of the novel, must
sometimes go to implausible lengths to learn about
goings-on involving Tacey, Gaye, and Seely. But the
first-person narration, whatever its inherent difficul-
ties, is essential to the writer's purpose; it demon-
strates, with directness and economy, Nugget's
growth in self-knowledge and in sympathetic aware-
ness of those who surround him.

One phase of the narrator's initiation into adulthood is his recognition of the falsity of the dream
of the "golden West" that lures him from his
Kansas home. As an eight-year-old boy in eastern
Kansas, Nugget can lie in his bed and "see through
the crabapple tree a luminous light in the western
sky." Following that light into New Mexico and
Arizona, he finds it "false as a gypsy." The narrative
that Nugget relates is set roughly in the first decade
of the twentieth century, well past the year 1890,
which, according to Frederick Jackson Turner's

famous dictum, marked the close of the American frontier. In the West, then, Nugget discovers, not the anarchic freedom and empty spaces celebrated in myth and legend, but a formative society very much like that found in the remainder of turn-of-the-century America. The sad fact that the legendary West no longer exists (if it ever did) is signaled for Nugget by the appearance of Andy Coe, a lawman who had once fought it out with famed south-western badmen; now, in 1900, he is an old man, the "marshal" of Bisbee, Arizona—really just the "town constable, subject to the whim of small politi-cians. . . ."

Rather than the mythic West, Nugget encoun-ters in the mining town of Bisbee the sometimes grim, sometimes exuberant reality of industrialized America. In Bisbee nature's resources—copper, in this instance—are furiously exploited by rich and poor alike. Accidental death, caused by appalling working conditions, is common. On the other hand Horatio Alger–esque men of thrift and hustle and good fortune are still possible in such a place (Senator Watrous, one of the town's richest citi-zens, had begun as a lowly miner). A roll call of miners who live in Brewery Gulch (they have names like Kushto, Farlaquatti, Michovich, Mac-Cachy, and O'Dell) suggests the flavor of the town's melting-pot society. Bisbee's population, it seems, is not much different from that of dozens of coal-mining towns in the author's native Pennsylvania.

The historical and social fabric woven by Richter in *Tacey Cromwell* is an extraordinarily rich one. In all his novels the writer took pains to establish those "endless, small authenticities," as he called them, that create in the reader's mind a strong sense of reality. And in realism of background *Tacey Cromwell* is one of the best of his narratives. For his "authenticities" Richter drew from information supplied by a friend, a geologist familiar with the history, social mores, and topography of the Bisbee area. Also the writer undoubtedly consulted files of the Bisbee *Review*, a newspaper that began publication in 1898. He used the results of careful research—real place names and historical events. The great fire, for example, which is the novel's climactic event, is a fictionalized version of a disastrous fire that actually occurred in Bisbee on October 14, 1908.

Richter's triumph in *Tacey Cromwell*, however, is not the accuracy of the story's historical backdrop, but his imaginative and totally believable reconstruction of the society of early twentieth-century Bisbee. Nugget turns out to be the ideal observer of that social structure, for he is allowed to move on every level of it—from Brewery Gulch to Quality Hill to the Watrous mansion. To Nugget the town is a "stage, with painted wings and scenery and always actors moving across it. It was a show you never tired of seeing." Richter's artistry in portraying Bisbee society is illustrated by the subtle balances and contrasts he sets up. In this regard, the reader should compare Bee Hosmer's simple home wedding with the expensive, ceremonious marriage of Gaye and Rudith; he should also compare the rowdy "funeral" of Seely Dowden's father with the genteel and very sedate burial of Miss Rudith. As Richter convincingly shows, the various forms given to such durable human institutions as marriage and burial are unfailing barometers of social values.

Nugget's increasingly clear-eyed and knowledgeable view of his home town is a gauge of his growing maturity. But the crucial aspect of his initiation is personal rather than social: it is his relationship with Tacey Cromwell. Though Nugget is the central figure in the novel, because it is, after all, his story—his initiation into life—Tacey is the title character of the book, as well as the focal point, in one way or another, of every incident in the plot. Several reviewers and commentators have condemned Richter's characterization of Tacey, claiming a lack of sufficient motivation for her abrupt shift from bawdy-house madam to "mother" and respectable businesswoman. In Tacey, Richter attempted to dramatize a historical fact: that most of the prostitutes and dance-hall girls of the old West eventually went legitimate, became wives and mothers—often happy and successful ones. Richter once said, in justifying Tacey's success as "mother" and Miss Rudith's failure in the same role, that "more intelligence in bringing up children is found in the once sporting house woman than in the soft loving mother brought up in luxury and ease." This seems, so far as it goes, a reasonable explanation, but it is nevertheless true that Tacey's behavior, particularly her sudden conversion to respectability, is never wholly explicable to the reader, because it is never wholly explicable to the narrator (nor probably to the author, for that matter). The first time Nugget sees her, Tacey provokes in him an "inkling of the

vague, secret, restless and mysterious things men
lacked and which never let them go." To Nugget
she appears to embody the female principle, and
that principle, for males anyway, stubbornly refuses
to submit itself to logical analysis.

As a child Nugget goes west on the trail of a
myth. An orphan, he also goes in search of Gaye,
his older half-brother who, he hopes, will serve as a
substitute father. He finds instead a substitute
mother, Tacey. Tacey's discipline, self-reliance, and
self-effacing loyalty to her "family" are truly heroic—
and perhaps, as some critics contend, not altogether
believable. Still, without such qualities she could
never have psychologically survived the Bisbee
ladies' puritanical ire; without them surely she could
not have continued to direct, with almost super-
human patience, the destinies of the people she
loves. Like Hester Prynne in *The Scarlet Letter*,
Tacey stoically endures social ostracism and little by
little faces down the "respectable" citizenry of an
entire town. Like Hester she acquires pleasure and
profit from sewing. Also like Hester she wins a
sizable, if largely private, victory over an inert public
morality that would have crushed a lesser person.

Nugget observes all this with growing admiration,
and in the end Tacey bestows on him the most
bountiful gift a parent can give a child: a model for
character building. Nugget learns, through Tacey,
that true strength of character is formed only in
the crucible of conflict and struggle. Things come
too easily for Rudith Watrous, for Gaye and Seely,
and their characters remain weak and indulgent.
Tacey suffers and endures and, as a result, becomes

a source of strength, a refuge, and a returning point for her beloved "family." The narrative ends with the family circle closed. Nugget comments that, in the beginning, "it had been Tacey and Seely and Gaye and I. Now here were the four of us again." One critic calls this "an improbable reunion." It seems to me, however, a necessary conclusion to Richter's characterization of Tacey, for her indomitable courage and determination are the elastic and unseen bonds that have drawn the family back together, have in a sense held it together all along.

Overall *Tacey Cromwell*, despite flaws, succeeds as a work of art because of its realistic and vivid portrayal of a southwestern town's social history and because it reveals, with warmth and sympathy, the generous spirit of a remarkable woman.

WILLIAM T. PILKINGTON
Tarleton State University
Stephenville, Texas

Contents

Chapter 1

THE LIGHT IN THE WEST

I WOULD rather say, if I could, that it was my step-
father and no blood of mine who made me leave
home so early, but that would be a lie. It was Wickers Covington, and that was almost the same as my
truly own father, for he was my father's closest
brother and the one after whom I was named. There
was a time when I hated him with all the poison of
a young rattlesnake. Now that I am older, I think
that perhaps he wasn't so much to blame. Nearly
everything he set his hand to turned out badly. He
couldn't stand it and tried to save himself by abus-
ing someone else. The deeper he went in, the more
he had to yell to support and convince himself. Soon
he was so far gone that if anybody talked back, he
had to strike out in a wild effort to stop his own hurt,
and then he was a man gone crazy. Even on his good
days when he wanted to be pleasant to people in

town, a faint wolfish taint of his tantrums hung about him and strangers shrank away from him without quite knowing why.

But I knew, and so did many others. My half-brother, Gaye, couldn't stand him when he came, and left. Gaye and I had the same mother but he had the best of me. He knew her for twelve years and she died the night I was born. People said it was God's mercy she didn't live and see my father crushed in Hollenback's Quarry. They all told me how she kept a clean house, but I never knew it. Go through parts of Missouri, Arkansas, Oklahoma, Texas and New Mexico today and you will see small boys like I was then, boys with good English names and faces. They will stand up to you with manly backs and answer you straight. But follow them to where they live and you'll wonder how they ever came out of such places.

That was our home on Cat Creek in eastern Kansas after my mother lay in her weedy grave, and my Uncle Wickers came to take charge. We had two stories of logs clapboarded over and dark from the weather. On wet days it looked charred black. At first you'd think it had never been painted, but high up under the eaves where the rain had not yet washed it off, I had seen traces of yellow. I used to lie in the grass and wonder how fine it must have looked with the paint still on, with a glass light in every window and my mother's organ and flowered carpet in the front room. A neighbor woman told me she had come over once and seen my mother's penciled sign by the back porch saying, " Please scrape your boots! " When I knew the house, the bare floors

were muddy and the rotting old roof dipped like a
sway-back horse. Sometimes today when I pass a
door where cheap meat is cooking, it takes me back
to that house in eastern Kansas and I can see the
newspaper pictures pasted over the logs and chink-
ing and the unmade bed that during my time knew
neither sheets nor bolster cases. I can smell again
the sweaty, unwashed bedding and damp old plaster, the reek of rats' nests under the board floors, and
the suffocating stench of a closed-up room slept in
from dark to dawn with last night's excretions still
unemptied.

But don't think that a boy in such places had
nothing precious to visit him like a beautiful lady in
the night. Mine came past sundown on hot summer
Kansas evenings. After I had taken off my pants and
shirt and lain naked on the bed I could see through
the crabapple tree a luminous light in the western
sky. Exactly what there was about that light I can-
not say except that it was something against the
lonely night to come. Also, it was golden like the
house had been when my mother was here, and it
lay toward the West where I thought her spirit
would like to be, near Gaye in the territory of New
Mexico. From the age of five I had lived only for
the day to join him.

And yet I didn't know the day when it came. Our
hay was still on the ground, in the long narrow bottom that curved like a snath along Cat Creek. It grew
natural prairie grass as high as my head. When I was
a child they didn't make me work, but now I was
eight, going on nine, and though I was small, I could
make a boy of twelve today look sick. I had raked

the field myself with our rusty one-horse rake, then gone along with my uncle, each of us with a fork. He'd take one end of a row and I the other and we'd roll them up into haycocks. It was all dry and fine and ready to be brought in, and I had hitched up the team in the hay ladders myself when the rain began to pour.

Nothing I did in the house or barn the rest of that day was right. When I dropped the frying pan and broken eggs on the kitchen floor, a kick in my crotch sent me half paralyzed into the yellow mess. And then the only happiness I knew was the thought that his hay was still out in the rain. All my secret way from the house that night, with my bare feet stumbling in puddles, and wet bushes along the narrow road soaking me as I went, I prayed it would rain on his hay till it turned coal-black on the ground and that his wheat on the hill would sprout useless in the shock.

When finally I came down the last ridge and saw my Uncle Calhoun's house and barn in the early mist, I knew I had walked eighteen miles. Up on another ridge lay the deeply rutted road that movers took to the West, but my feet could hardly wait to turn in to my Uncle Calhoun's barn. He was my good uncle, on my mother's side, and his little black and tan dog, Tippy, came barking wildly out at me. Then he caught my smell and jumped up whining and licking at my face. When I crawled under the warm dry hay in the mow, he crawled under, too, his tail whipping, and he stayed with me most of the day, leaving me only to run and bark violently and importantly when some rig passed and then coming

back to burrow under to me again, faithful as if he
had chased off an army. I had bread stolen from our
house for us both, and Tippy never deserted me,
not even when they came to milk and feed. It rained
on the barn roof all day. Toward afternoon I thought
I heard the jog of our sorrel and the rattle of our rig
and was glad I hadn't gone to the house. Now my
Uncle Calhoun could say with honest surprise, why
no, he hadn't seen hide nor hair of me!

That night I stole up to the movers' road and two
or three miles beyond where they often camped for
the night in Bieber's woods. I coaxed Tippy along.
He must have thought we were just out for a walk
and that we would come back to my Uncle Calhoun's before morning. But when daylight came, he
and I were hidden under a wagon sheet that spiraled
in the back as if the wagon's eye looked out at people. There were two wagons, one with great spokes
and deep in the mud with a heavy load that wouldn't
be needed till they got there — the other a spring
wagon to carry the chuck and bedrolls. I could hear
two men and made up my mind what I'd say when
I came out. I would lie that I was ten, and that I had
come from across the Missouri, which would be too
far to send me home.

When the wheels started to move, Tippy licked
my face. I think he expected we were going back now
to his rusty old feed pan in my Uncle Calhoun's yard.
When the wheels stopped for noon he whined
eagerly. I'm sure he thought: Here we are at home
again. I can still smell his strong doggy odor under
the hot canvas and feel his small hard legs trying to
dig through the heavy tailboard of the wagon.

Chapter 2

TO THE LADIES

IT was a vaster universe across my home state than I had ever known along Cat Creek. Mornings and evenings the Gurleys made me rustle water and wood, look after the horses, and sand the greasy pans. But the rest of the day I had nothing to do but just sit like a rich man jolting in one of the wagons by strange new fields and dooryards. When the farms petered out, it was like getting in a new state, though the Gurleys grunted we were still in Kansas. No barns or fences here, only a kind of desert land. From the combs of the ridges you could see the deep ruts, ten and twenty abreast, running across an empire vast and empty as the sky. You could see the wheel tracks ahead for ten or fifteen miles. Everything told me I was getting closer to Gaye's country. This was out West where my brother lived. I didn't notice the heat or barren ground or that something had come over Tippy. He used to go chasing off the road after

every wandering smell. Now he kept silently in the
shade of the wagon I happened to be riding in, his
tongue hanging out and jerking faster than the eye
could follow.

We watered the horses at a lonely bend in the
Arkansas. Tippy waded in and flopped himself down
till only his nose stuck out. When we started off, he
was like his old self again, jumping, barking and
snapping at the noses of the horses.

" What's the matter with him? " the older Gurley
said sharply. " He's got white on his jaw."

" It's nothing the matter with him," I told him.
" Just foam off the river."

" That's no river foam! " Gurley shouted. He
stopped his team, wrapped the lines on the brake and
reached back in the wagon. " He'll give it to the
horses! "

" I often seen him like that, Mr. Gurley! " I
told him, jumping down in the trail. " I'll show you.
Here, Tippy, Tippy, Tippy! " I called.

At first I thought that Tippy was just full of life
and working it off. He had started running circles
around the teams and wagons. He had done this before when feeling good, but today when I called on
him to stop, he passed me by as if he had never known
me or slept cuddled up between my arms and belly.
It gave me a funny feeling. I saw now there was something a little strange in the way he held his head, not
forward, but back and a little to the side, while the
ears had a desperate cock. He ran as if rigid, almost
contorted. He acted scared of something. When he
swerved to the desert, I guessed he was leaving us
and tried to stop him. His circles were uncertain,

lopsided, working toward a far blue ridge that looked like some cool, watered and timbered hill on the horizon. But I knew that if he got there he would find it only barren desert like this, and I stumbled after him, calling and bawling.

I didn't see the two Gurleys till they came running up and one of them swung me from the ground.

" Let me go! " I fought with him as if he were my uncle.

The other Gurley knelt and laid his black beard along his rifle.

" You can't do that! " I screamed at him, kicking and scratching, but even so, down in my heart I never thought there was danger, for Tippy was just a speck on the desert. The rifle cracked and when they set me on my feet again, Tippy had disappeared. In all that expanse of solitude nothing moved. I wanted to run out there and look for him but they carried me bawling to the wagons.

We put in to camp just a mile or two beyond, and when they sent me to the river for wood I made a wide circle and ran nearly all the way back where Tippy had left the wagons. I could see where the horses had stood and the heavy tracks the Gurleys' boots made in the sand. The sun was an ominous red wheel on the desert when I found him, lying flatter than I had ever seen him in life. Blood had already dried on his short black and tan fur. I thought he was dead. When I called to him his closed lids never moved but I could tell he heard my voice, for after a moment I saw fresh blood answer faintly but unmistakably through the wound.

I never got over that. I carried him back to camp

in my arms. That night with the camp shovel I buried him, with sobs breaking out of my chest, water scalding my eyes, and hate for his murderers in my brain. We found out next day we were only three miles from the state line. Neither Tippy nor I had ever been out of Kansas in our lives. For a week I had been looking forward to it. Now when we crossed the line I couldn't look at it, thinking of Tippy. All the way through southeast Colorado I called myself ugly names for taking him away from a good home, and never even giving him the pleasure of seeing another state but leaving him in a God-forsaken desert with no dogs but wild ones for a hundred miles.

At Trinidad, where the trails forked, I left them without a word of thanks, only curses on the one who had murdered Tippy. And from then on I was a kind of camp dog myself, begging rides where I could and starving, first with one movers' outfit and then another. Kansas and Colorado I remember like the scar from a knife. But the Raton of New Mexico is a blur to me like Oldtown in Las Vegas and the Indians in Santa Fe. All that kept me going was the picture in my mind of Socorro ahead where my brother lived. The wagon road then ran on the east bank of the Rio Grande and I thought it would never end. Twice the wagons broke down. The day they said they'd surely get to Socorro, they only crossed the river bridge and reached a feathery tamarisk bottom still some miles away. The sunset was already dead behind the furry trees and bushes when I sneaked off.

I can still feel myself that chunk of a boy, not

much higher than the rear wheel of a wagon, starting
down the unknown desert valley trail. It was darker
off from the camp fires than I had figured, and much
lonelier. The sounds of the camp grew fainter, and
the desert came up through the clear dimness all
around. Far as I could see, no lights broke the solitude. Behind and on either side, shadowy spaces
swallowed me up like a fly. Ahead, dark mountains
shaped like arrowheads reached up and blacked out
the stars. The only smell my nose could get in this
dry country was the faint creosote stink of grease-
wood. It was all strange enough to a boy from eastern Kansas and I felt I had come pretty far from that
house on Cat Creek bottom. Only the sand, still
warm to my feet, was like something I had known
before.

It seemed very late when I came to my brother's
town. My feet felt their way up a street of silent
cottonwoods where all seemed to be dark and asleep,
and out into a square where lamps in glass signs made
the boardwalks bright as moonlight. This, I told
myself, must be the golden West at last where people
had more money than they could spend in the daytime. The hour was after midnight, but the business
houses stood open as at noon. I saw a busy restaurant,
a barber shop, a bakery, a drug store, a hardware
store, and lamps burning in a justice of the peace
office. I saw a white-cheeked man shoulder sack after
sack of flour out of an establishment marked Gen-
eral Merchandise and dump it in a sheeted wagon.
Open-air lunch stands stood among the racked horses
and the rich smells of boiling coffee and beefsteak
gravy made my tongue thicken.

Men were everywhere, although I couldn't see a woman. I stopped a big man in leather boots who had pushed out of an assayer's office.

" Gaye Oldaker? " He squinted down at my vest and my coat that reached the worn places at the knees of my long pants. " What in hell do you want with him? "

" He's my half-brother," I told him proudly.

"You'll find him at the White Palace," he grunted. " But you better wait till tomorrow to see him."

I waited only till he had gone, then I started looking around the square for a white building like the Methodist church in Tomsville, Kansas. I went around twice, spelling out every sign, but no White Palace was there. Later I found if off the square and half a block wide.

Since then I have been back and seen it by day, a dingy, one-story mud building half washed away by rains and standing in an alley. But that night it awed me to my bones. When the door opened, it was like peeping into Ali Baba's cave with brass lamps swinging through rich tobacco smoke. The shining bar was loaded with glittering glasses and veritable haycocks of things to eat, while small tables stood stacked with gold and silver and red, white, and blue chips.

When a rancher pushed in, I went right after, trying not to be overwhelmed, looking for someone like the picture of my brother, three years old, in a dress, with his thumb stuck into an unimpressed mouth. Nobody like that was there. I remembered hearing that Gaye could play my mother's organ, but the face of the piano player here was old and battered, and no brother of mine would lower himself to a violin. The bartenders looked too high and mighty; as did the men in smoking jackets and aprons, who I know now ran the craps table, faro bank, and monte table. And the youngish fellow at the wheel was too grand for a brother of mine, in a brown suit, no apron; and his brown hat, instead of hanging on a nail, tilted away from a shrewd unreadable face.

So far there had been only men in this Rio Grande town. Now I glimpsed my first women, most of them dancing, talking, or drinking with men, none in the short skirts and low waists of later days, all of them dressed like any other women I knew, only better. I thought they were the ladies of Socorro decked out in their Sunday finery and my heart beat proud that my brother should work in such a fine place.

" Hul-lo! " a girl's voice said right behind me.

I turned and saw it wasn't a girl but a woman in a green silk dress and bright green ribbons in her hair. Her face, to my astonishment, now that I was close to her, had been powdered and painted like a circus clown's.

" Ain't he something! " she said admiringly to the man with her. Then to me: " What you doing here, honey? "

" I'm looking for somebody," I told her, hard as I could.

" And who might that somebody be? " she coaxed.

" Gaye Oldaker," I said, bowing my back. " He's my half-brother."

I saw with fierce pride that the name meant something.

" Never knew Gaye had a brother," the man said.

" Well, why don't you go over and talk to him, honey? " the woman said.

" I ain't never seen him," I admitted, flushing.

The man looked meaningly at the woman but she bent down till her face was almost up against mine.

" Don't he know you're here, honey? "

" I just got in," I told her. " I run off from Kansas same as he did."

" Well, ain't that something! " she said again admiringly. " And no bigger'n a minute! " She turned to the man. " You wait, deary, I'll take him in to Tacey."

She gripped my hand in her limy, white one studded with rings and large freckle spots, and we started toward the dance floor. But before we had gone twenty feet, women were crowded around laughing and wouldn't let me through.

" Ain't he the cute little feller? "

" Where'd you get him, Kate? "

" He's mine."

" No, he's mine."

" He's spunkier than a banty rooster."

They hauled and mauled and pushed and nudged me over to a corner where I fought to get free from this one and to avoid that one's reeking breath.

" Let him go, you bitches! " the woman called Kate yelled at them. " I'm taking him in to Tacey."

" She only reckons she is," a plump little woman in bright red said. " Here comes the madam now."

Chapter 3

TACEY

BETWEEN the skirts reeking of perfume and powder, I saw this person called Tacey coming from a rear door. She was slight, her face almost pale, but you couldn't miss her. Her plain black tailored dress with its lace collar and cuffs stood out severely from all the fancy reds, yellows, and greens. She looked very proper and genteel except for her yellow, almost orange-colored hair, which appeared to have been stained or bleached with acid. Staring at that artificial and licentious shade and then at the circumspect rest of her gave you the feeling that here was a being of strange, conflicting forces. I was only a boy eight years old going on nine and she gave me my first inkling of the vague, secret, restless and mysterious things men lacked and which never let them go. Even today when I think of her as she was then, perhaps a little crude and make-believe, yet

young, ambitious, and intense, a current of vitality
and faint excitement warms me and brings back the
very feel of that whisky, tobacco, and scent-ridden
room.

A prominent-looking drinker had moved across
the floor to talk to her, a man with an extraordinary
paunch which he guided with dignity ahead of him,
shifting it carefully from one leg to the other.

At the sight of him and Tacey together, Kate had
halted.

" Look at those sleeves! " she jeered to another
woman. " She's changed them again. That's six
times. She set them four times till they suited her
in the first place."

The woman, who had pink ribbons crossed over
her ankles, turned her head.

" What's wrong with changing them if she wants
to? That's the new style. She read it in the paper."

Kate ignored her and went on loudly.

" She comes from some little old ranch down in
Texas or the Nations. But she got the idea she's a
lady and can boss me around."

" The judge thinks so, too," the woman in pink
said. " He's telling her to keep you and your red
stockings off the streets Sunday afternoons."

Kate snorted, let go of my hand, and started belligerently across the floor. I saw her break boldly into
the talk and point her limy, ring-ridden hand at
me. The judge's slow impassive glance passed over
us but the eyes of Tacey glowed and burned at me
with a green fire of unwelcome. I stared back as
hard and defiant as I could.

Kate came back grumbling and grabbed my hand.

" I'm to take you the hell out of here."

I thought she meant out on the street.

" Let go or I'll tell my brother! " I fought her, kicking and squirming.

Before she had yanked me half-way across the floor, men and women were jeering at her, calling her a cradle-robber and making jokes about her crib which I didn't understand. She was a match for any and all of them, brawling right back and raising plenty of laughs. Then we passed through the shadowy door in the partition.

I found we were in a long narrow hall lighted by occasional bracket lamps. These left it rather dim but I could see that each one of the long row of doors had a name painted on it. I remember afterward there were Midnight Rose and Drowsy Dolly, Wee Bee, Darling Etta, Babe, Fleabitten Daisy, and Rowdy Kate. In most cases only the last name was in paint and the other added in ink or pencil. I wanted to go slow and spell them out, but she pulled me along past them and by a sheepish-looking man making his way alone to the dance floor.

" Well, did you see her pitchers! " Kate snapped at him.

At the end we halted in front of a door without a painted name, and no one had added any. This she unlocked.

" Now you go in and stay in! " She seemed to hold me responsible for everything and pushed me in and slammed the door.

I stood very still. It was the finest room I had ever seen, with an elegant brass bed and red blanket

folded at the foot. Most everything in the room
was red — the cushions on the couch, the long hang-
ings at the window, and the thin curtains that covered one corner for a closet where I saw that a man's
clothes as well as a woman's hung. Even the shade
of the turned-down lamp was red, throwing its peculiar light over a large account book open on the
small table and on two pictures tucked in the mirror
of the marble-top bureau.

I moved closer to look at those pictures. One was
the youngish dealer in the high hat I had seen at the
wheel. The other was a girl of twelve in a new
fancy dress standing in front of an unpainted house.
Who she was I didn't know but there seemed to
be something familiar about her eyes. Then the dark
crockery knob turned behind me and when I looked
around, I was staring at the lady they called Tacey.

She came in slowly, her eyes on me bright and
hard. Now that she was close I could see that she
had painted herself like the other women, only less
so. Her lip was a red scar and the pink in her cheeks
made her look burning.

" Why did you come here? "

I just stared at her, not knowing what to do or
say.

" How did you come? " she went on.

" On the wagons."

" Why did you run off? Does your uncle know
where you are? "

At the sudden mention of my uncle, something
in me flared.

" He kicked me in the crotch! "

She bent to raise the red flannel wick of the lamp.

" Well, nobody will kick you here," she said briefly. One of her hands turned up the gold watch that hung over her breast. " It's time for a kid like you to be in bed."

" I want to see my brother," I defied her.

" He'll be here in the morning."

" It's morning now."

" I mean daylight."

" Do you know him? " I asked.

" Know Caye Oldaker? " Her eyes got very hard. " Have you anything along? A nightgown? "

I shook my head.

" You'll have to sleep in one of Gaye's shirts." Her hand laid back the covers, and sight of real white sheets made me stare.

" I washed all over in the river tonight," I told her. " I had no soap. But I had sand! " I added as if that was just as good.

There must have been marks aplenty of a thousand miles of travel still on me, and she couldn't help seeing them, for she helped me off rapidly with my shoes as if the sooner I was in bed, the sooner she'd be done with me. I tried to hold back but the quick deft way she knelt down and undid the lacers showed she must have had young brothers at home and done this many times before. I kept telling myself all the time I wouldn't let her or any other woman touch me, but she went ahead so swiftly and impersonally I didn't know what I was doing. When her hands pulled off my pants, I pushed my shirt down far as it would go, which wasn't far because it was more like a blouse and wasted no cloth on tails. I stood there feeling mighty sick, but she only gave

me an enigmatic look, pulled a shirt much too large
over me and pinned back the sleeves.

Gingerly I got in between the white sheets.

" Does it matter which side? " I stammered.

" No," she said briefly and I could tell by that I
wouldn't be sleeping here long.

I reached for the covers, but she pulled them up
herself and laid them around my unaccustomed
shoulders. She stood for a moment looking down at
me. I couldn't make out whether her red scar of a
lip curved or curled. Then her fingers turned down
the lamp and I could hear her unseen petticoats
swish out.

I must have slept very uneasily in that strange,
red-lighted place, for low voices woke me. With eyes
still closed I peered out through my lashes. It was
gray morning and a man stood over me. He had on
a long white nightshirt with red stitches and it took
a while for me to recognize him without his bright
brown suit and brown hat as the man at the roulette wheel. Even in his nightshirt his face looked
unreadable, although his hands against the white
gown were brown and capable.

" So that's little Wick? " he said sardonically.

" He says his name's Nugget Oldaker," Tacey
told him.

I watched the man throw back his head, but no
laughter came. Only the humorous lines deepened
in his face.

" His name's Wickers Covington. Same as his
uncle's. Looks like he don't want anything to do
with the old devil."

" He doesn't look much like you."

"No, and maybe I better not sleep with him. Him and me might get to fighting like the old man." The nightshirted figure crossed the room in his bare feet to the red couch that wasn't red any more. Someone had fixed it up into a bed with sheets and blankets.

To my right I could see Tacey standing over a large white bowl on the wash stand, wiping paint intently off her face with a folded cloth. She looked taller in her long, muslin nightdress with ruffles and pink tatting at its wrists and high neck. Her orange-colored hair hung in low braids over her shoulders. I had never seen a woman prepared for bed before, and she seemed a revelation to me, softer and very different from her other self. But I couldn't help noticing the quick pitiless way her white hands wrung out the washcloth.

"You haven't said what you're going to do about it, Gaye." She spoke with low passion.

I saw him raise a sober and appraising glance, but no words came from him.

"Well, he can't stay here!" she promised, dashing the water into the slop jar.

I was fully awake now and watched the other closely, hanging on his reply. I couldn't believe yet that he was my brother. He looked nothing like the Gaye Oldaker in my mind and acted less. He must have known well enough what would happen to me if they shipped me home, yet he let himself be backed down by a woman. She stood there dangerously, challenging him, waiting to fly into the next things he'd say. But he wouldn't fight with her, not even for me. He just stretched himself out, his face

a little puckered and rueful like Uncle Calhoun's
after a go with Aunt Jo back in Kansas.

" Have it your way, Tacey," he said, and turned,
pulling the covers after him, so all I could see now
was a patch of his dark, straight hair.

I tried to keep my lip steady. It seemed it wasn't
right that I had come hundreds of miles, footed it
through rain and sand, fought, gone hungry, drunk
mud for water, and after I got here, I couldn't stay.
Thoughts of Tippy, the only true friend I ever had,
came and I had to keep my eyes tightly shut to keep
the pillow from staining. That golden Western
light, I could see now, was false as a gypsy. It might
look bright enough back in Kansas. But once you
were close, it came through the window gray and
mocking.

Tacey moved around the footboard like a woman
who had won a victory. I felt her getting into bed
behind me. She got in softly as if not to disturb me,
but my small legs drew away from her side as far as
they were able. I'd have given either one of them
to be back right then with the wagons.

But when the sun woke me, I wasn't so sure. It
looked golden again streaming through the red curtains. Something I never knew before had been
thrown over my shoulder. By careful touch I found
it was a soft arm in long-sleeved muslin. This person, Tacey, must have curved herself around my
small body as I slept and now lay breathing so
lightly she didn't seem to weigh down the bed at
all. What astonished me was that anyone could
sleep there so peacefully with the sun high in the
sky.

Despite myself a slow warmth crept over me. I scarcely breathed so as not to wake her. She lay close to me as a sister. I had never stayed in a woman's house before, let alone slept in her bed. Gaye snored only a few feet away. I knew now he might not stick by me like I expected. This might be only for the night. But I was united with my half-brother at last.

Chapter 4

THE ROCK

THAT week in the White Palace was the happiest I had known until then. The cook teased me and fed me tidbits. The baker's boy picked a fight with me in the kitchen with most of the house taking my side. The butcher, when he came to collect his weekly bill from Tacey, gave me a Mexican two-bit piece.

Most of the women liked me and tried to get me to visit them of an afternoon in their rooms. There they'd sit, two or three together, in their loose wrappers. I had never even heard of a woman smoking cigarettes before and it shocked me a little at first. But they all did it, even Tacey, I think, though I never caught her at it. There was something unbelievably daring to see them sit there and puff and then hold the cigarette lazily between their fingers as if they were sharing with me some secret and fascinating vice.

Endearing talk ran from them free and easy as water from an irrigation ditch. They told me Gaye used to be the piano player but Tacey had got him the wheel job. They said that one afternoon he and Mr. Taggart, the proprietor, were going out for a buggy ride. Mr. Taggart forgot his gloves, and while he went back for them, Gaye bucked the faro game and won seventy dollars from the house. After that Mr. Taggart always called those gloves his seventy-dollar gloves.

But the story I listened to the hardest was the one where two Magdalena men had killed each other in the White Palace. They had come to Socorro just to settle it between them and went to bucking Gaye's game. When the shooting started, they followed each other around, keeping the wheel between them. One fired five shots and the other six. Two bullets went through the wheel. Most everybody in the place threw himself to the floor, but Gaye sat quiet on the stool between them. " It wasn't nerve," he said afterward. " Sitting still was the safest thing to do. They knew where I was at. If I had jumped around, they might have plugged me." But it made me warm with pride for my brother.

Sometimes the women looked to see that Tacey wasn't around, then gave me a draw on their cigarettes. I had to crawl up on their laps to get it and they'd try to keep me there, fussing over and fondling me. But the minute I got my smoke, I'd fight away from the feel of their soft arms and breasts.

"Ain't he the little squirmer! " they'd tell each other admiringly.

" Look at his hands — no bigger'n a pet coon's! "

" That's a lie! " I'd tell them.

" Just feel his muscle, Bee."

" Spunky as his half-brother, ain't he? "

" And now he's lighting out. Don't you like us, honey? "

" You're all right," I told them stiffly.

" Then what are you dragging Gaye and Tacey off for? " they coaxed me.

My face stayed dead as Gaye's at his wheel but inside of me a great joy rose. That was the first I knew that I wasn't going off alone.

After three or four days Tacey brought a strange woman into her room to teach her how to keep the account books. She dropped no hint to me of what it meant, and Gaye's only confidings were long, silent, almost unfriendly shots from his eyes, as if he were studying something out. He left two new, stylish kind of valises called suitcases in the room, and I thought it wouldn't be long now. The pleasant leather smell was still there that evening but Tacey's iron-bound trunk was gone. Next morning when I awoke, Tacey had already dressed in her best. Looking over where Gaye had slept I saw it was a red couch again, and that the new clothes they had bought for me were laid out with care across it.

When Tacey and I got out in the hall, the women ran to their open doors to see us go. Such a bleary-eyed and touseled crew in nightgowns and wrappers I've never laid eyes on since.

" Good-by! "

" Good luck to you, Tacey."

" Hope you and Gaye do well, kid."

"Don't forget us, Tacey, honey."

"When you're settled, deary, drop us a line."

Wee Bee, the only one I ever saw Tacey take in her room, hugged her like a sister. When I looked back, some of them had gone, but Rowdy Kate still stood in her doorway like some mournful, hollow-eyed hawk, beaked and fiercely predatory.

"Make the son-of-a-bitch marry you!" she called hoarsely after.

It was the first time I had ever seen Tacey outside the White Palace, and almost before the door closed behind her she changed and stiffened. In the glaring sunlight of the alley she might have been someone I had never seen before, with unpainted cheeks and lips, her new suit trimmed with fine gray fur, and hat with a tall feather.

The day was Saturday and the square, when we got to it, was filled with teams and people. I expected others to bid Tacey good-by and wondered why nobody spoke to her. I saw the judge who had talked to her in the White Palace look the other way. Watching women nudged one another to look and spoke low, guarded words I couldn't catch. In front of them Tacey moved with a strange deliberate gait, holding herself higher and more tightly than in the White Palace. She might have been the only person on the street. But I noticed that when she passed close to the whispering women, one of her hands swung stiffly out of control.

The brick bank grew silent when we came in.

"I want to take it all out," Tacey said in a low voice at the window.

The banker didn't speak to her either. He moved

gravely to a high desk, opened a thick book, wrote something on a small piece of paper, and pushed it at her over the counter. Tacey put the thick layer of bills and the heavy gold pieces into her crocheted bag. At the station she told me to stay with her satchel in the waiting-room. Outside I could see her walking up and down.

After the train left Socorro, Gaye came in from the smoking car carrying the two suitcases. He put them up in the rack and then turned a seat to ride backward. Several times I saw him scrutinize Tacey silently. When the brakeman came through, lighting the oil lamps with a taper on a stick, she leaned back and closed her eyes. For a long time Gaye stared out of the black window, his lips and cheeks set thoughtfully. Today I know this was an event in their lives, a step to take when they didn't have to, and no one could tell what would come out of it.

I remember being helped by a brakeman off a second train the next evening and seeing what I thought were huge stars in the sky. They hung high above me, spattering the blackness, and one or two were red. I had never seen any red stars before and I kept staring at them as I stumbled along after Tacey. As my sight improved, perpendicular walls of rock loomed out of the darkness and I found that what I had thought stars were the lights of houses perched high on the cliffs overhead.

We went uptown on a very high boardwalk and Tacey stopped near the dimly lighted sign of the Vendome Hotel. Today I know that for all its three brick stories and Main Street location, it was a shabby old place even then and something in me

winces at the thought of Tacey standing nervous
and hesitant in front of it.

"You got to be careful," Gaye reminded quietly.

"We're four hundred miles from Socorro!" Tacey whispered.

As if riding her impulse before it would ebb, she
led the way quickly inside. I had never been in a
hotel lobby in my life, not even a dim one like this,
and the men I supposed to be drummers sitting on
the leather chairs impressed me. Under their bold
scrutiny I saw Tacey stiffen and her arm fling as in
Socorro. At the desk she waited nervous and intense
for the clerk, who merely turned a large open account book toward her and handed her a pen, holder
first, after dipping it in a smeared black bottle. What
she was to write with the pen I had no idea, but I
saw her eye run quickly over lines others had written
ahead of her. Then the pen clasped in her gloved
thumb and forefinger rode in little stylish circles
across the page.

"I would like two rooms," she said in a low voice.

They seemed very large and grand to me when we
got there, with their high ceilings and heavy, ancient, black furniture. I was put in with Gaye and
understood that for some reason I wasn't to sleep
with Tacey here. With his hat still on, Gaye kept
walking up and down till a quick, genteel tapping
sounded on the door and Tacey slipped in.

"This is pretty tony stuff, Cromwell," he said.

"It's not too tony for me," she told him.

"One room was enough for us in Socorro."

"It might be here," Tacey said quietly, "if we
were señor and señora."

Something in her voice made me look at her. She had taken off her hat and coat in her room, perhaps brushed her hair a little, and washed the soot from her cheeks. But it wasn't that. She stood there watching him, her green eyes enigmatic as before except that now underneath there was something else, something almost eager rising in her. It wasn't quite up as yet where you could see it. Then Gaye turned his back and I felt it harden like shellac.

" I'll run uptown and look things over," he said. " Tell you about it when I get in."

" Tell me tomorrow." Her voice sounded suddenly a little thin. " I'm going to bed."

" Why, it's only ten or eleven o'clock."

" I've got to get used to sleeping nights. I might as well start now."

This copper-mining town, Bisbee, turned out bigger by day than I had any idea of. The houses stood packed for two miles along the narrow, winding canyon street and the rocky hills above. Tacey had routed me out early from beside Gaye, who hadn't come in till nearly daylight. I hadn't had much rest on the train and fought sleepily to stay in my warm bed.

" I want you along, Nugget! " she said.

Why she wanted me she didn't say, but I noticed as we went down the stairs and out to a restaurant for breakfast that she kept me very close. Once when I wanted to run across the street to see a burro with a pack saddle, she asked me in a low voice to stay with her. Before she went in anywhere to inquire about a house for rent or stopped people to ask for directions, she took my hand. Everyone smiled to me and was very polite to her, and after a while I noticed her other hand didn't swing out of control any more, even when we went up to men.

It was mid afternoon when we got back to the hotel. Gaye stood bent over his bureau shaving, wiping his razor on squares of newspaper and applying smaller pieces to his face to stick there and staunch the cuts. His face looked like a store shutter all tagged with snuff and chewing-tobacco signs.

" This damn water! " he said. " Did you find a room? "

" I wasn't looking for any," Tacey told him. " Can I rest on your bed a minute? " She stretched out, a little kitty-cornered, eyes closed and fluttering slightly, her very fine, dusty, high-button shoes sticking out over the ingrain carpet.

He threw her a look that told he wondered but wouldn't ask her any more.

" I was looking for a house," she said, her eyes still closed.

" A house? " he demanded.

Tacey said nothing more till she sat up.

" Nugget and I better go up awhile," she told him. She found the baggage check for the trunk in her purse and gave it to him. " Tell the drayman we live in Brewery Gulch."

Gaye gave her a stare.

" Up on O.K. Street," Tacey went on. " I'll be out on the porch. Don't you think that name's a good sign? "

" I think you're crazy," Gaye told her, starting grimly to pick the slips of paper from his face.

From the front porch where Tacey had stationed me to watch for Gaye, I saw him riding up Brewery Gulch with the drayman. Although they were far below me, I thought I could see Gaye staring around him with amazement. I didn't blame him. Brewery Gulch was the most astounding place. The horse toiled up the narrow street that clung so desperately and miraculously to the side of the cliff. I wondered that people had ever come up here to live, yet the whole gulch was inhabited, like a vast amphitheater, with houses hanging like wasps' nests one above the other all around the horseshoe of tall cliffs.

The late fall sunshine warmed the eastern side and here and there a man or two stood motionless on their lofty doorsteps taking in the scene. High up on the great precipice a girl took down wash in a tiny yard held aloft by log cribbing. In a still higher garden a woman dug out turnips and you knew that the soil of that terraced garden must have been carried up the long steps bucketful by bucketful. Somewhere an unseen player practiced on his cornet. Boys ran and played where a misstep would mean death. Across the gulch on a double boarding-house porch an unknown flag hung beside the Stars and Stripes. Today must be some foreigners' holiday.

The dray had reached the end of the street now. Beyond was no more than a trail and I called to Tacey, who came out. She looked steely efficient in the skirt, waist, and shoes she had rolled into her hand satchel.

" This is the place! " she called down in her best soprano.

It took them a long while to get up the trunk. The long flight of wooden steps over the cliff groaned and trembled.

" In here, Gaye! " she ordered competently when they reached the little box of a front porch. " Under this window. It'll be a window seat."

When the drayman had clumped down with his money, I saw Gaye staring around. You could guess he didn't think much of this whole business, still less of Tacey thinking she would stay in a miner's cabin. Most of the furniture hadn't been taken out because it couldn't be. The beds were wooden bunks. The tables, cupboard, bureau, settee, and chest of drawers had been built into the walls. Evidently the melodeon, benches, and curious, slanting-board chairs hadn't been worth an auction by themselves. All were whittled out of pine, carved with home-made curlicues. Not a stitch of carpet lay on the floor.

" What do you think of it? " Tacey called from the kitchen.

" What do you? " was all Gaye said, with his back toward her as she hurried in with the key to the trunk. From it she kept lifting things. The bunk in the front room she covered with a genteel afghan she had crocheted herself. It had a scalloped edge and was bright as a deck of cards. On the wooden settee she laid a smartly embroidered pillow. She hung a piece of gold velvet on one bare front wall and a bunch of brilliant green and bronze ostrich feathers on the opposite. A runner with long tassels went on the scrubbed front table and on this a tiny red lamp she wouldn't be able to light tonight because the oil had been drained to pack. Beside the lamp she laid an elegant pile of books, the *English Speaker* in orange cloth; *The Ladies' Companion* in red paper covers; and a fashion magazine with smooth heavy paper and a French name. Other things still flowed from the trunk, the last a piece of pure white fur which she shook out and laid on the bare board floor. It wasn't much bigger than two feet could stand on, yet it gave a touch of luxury to the room.

I had to help Tacey in the sleeping-room and when I came out Gaye had taken off his coat and sat down at the melodeon. It was a wooden box scarcely above his waist, painted a dull yellow and with a very short keyboard. I thought he made a picture sitting there, his knees moving up and down, his head on one side and brown hat tilted back. I had never heard him play before. Tacey sent me away before he was done, down once for water, down again for wood, and down to the store for coffee and milk lunch crackers.

We ate supper silently in the kitchen. Afterward Gaye lit a cigar and combed his hair.

"Think I'll run downtown and try to rustle up something." He said it offhand but the little volleys of smoke side-firing with the words shot out confidently. It seemed very strange to me, going out at night to look for a job.

"Take a wheel job for a while if you have to," Tacey told him. "But remember, what you want to get in is faro."

Gaye gave her a look as he put on his coat, one eye closed from the smoke.

" I mean it! " she warned him. " We're going to be respectable here in Bisbee."

" I never even worked at faro," he said, almost angrily. " Any floorman could tell it."

" Then get a layout and practice."

I was impressed. Back in Socorro when anyone said " the bank," he meant faro. In the White Palace a faro banker carried more respect than a regular banker. Indeed, I thought those days that faro was spelled Pharaoh as in the Bible.

Gaye's mouth was set in repressed rebellion.

" Now, if any floorman asks where you live," Tacey told him when he left, " don't say Brewery Gulch. Say O.K. Street. Or Youngblood Hill! "

Chapter 5

YOUNGBLOOD HILL

I HAD noticed her standing behind her door the first
day I had climbed the steps. All I could make out
then was a kid as big as I, a shag of hair, and that she
was watching me. The next day when I came home,
Tacey was away. I sat on our steps in the sun warming myself. Pretty soon the girl next door came out
and began silently skinning the cat on her rough
front-porch rail.

Her house — it wasn't more than a cabin — hung
from the same ledge on the cliff as ours, but no
boardwalk lay between and that gave me some satisfaction. I knew why she had come out, and when
she started to show off, I turned my back. Now that
I saw her in the daylight I hadn't much use for her.
Her dress had a dirty gray look that reminded me of
our unwashed things on Cat Creek. When she hung

by her knees, it came down around her neck, and you could see that her legs were crusty.

I knew she couldn't hurt herself if she fell. Their tiny terraced yard lay beneath. But after I wouldn't look, she went over to the gulch side and hung by her legs where there wasn't anything but a hundred and fifty feet to the trail below. That made me half mad. I had been out here taking it easy in the sun and she had to come out and bother me. I sneaked a look out of the corner of my eye, and when she saw it she began lifting her arms as if trying to get up and then falling back as if she couldn't make it. I knew it was just for my benefit and stood it as long as I could.

" You can break your neck for all I care! " I called out at last.

She paid no attention except to hang deliberately by her toes.

" Go on and kill yourself if you want to! " I yelled.

She said nothing, just kept her upside-down eyes fastened on me and took one foot from the rail.

" If you want to show off, get some pants! " I called to her.

She put her foot back slowly and I knew that I had her.

" Get some pants! " I jeered at her. " You don't have nothing on! "

She pulled herself up by her hands and stood on the porch.

" You better cover 'em up! " I taunted in triumph. " You're knock-kneed as an old mare! "

She sprang down the steps, reached for a rock, and let fly at me. She threw with a funny underhand mo-

tion, but the rock struck the porch close to my
head. I had to jump down and fire one at her to be
even. Right then I thought she might call it quits,
but I didn't know her. She threw another and so
did I. Pretty soon it was what in mining camps they
call a rock battle. She stayed on her steps and I
stayed on mine, but we had to keep going lower
down all the time for more rocks. Not a word passed
between us now. I could see her mouth closed like a
small trap and her eyes narrowed to dam back the
hate for me.

Down on the last flight she threw wild. The rock
sailed over my head and down the steep bank across
the narrow trail. A moment later came the jangle of
glass.

" Yippy — 'ippy — 'ippy — 'ippy! " I yelled with
delight, dancing up and down. It made her so mad
her next rock caught me under the chin. When I
took my hand away I saw it was dripping with
blood.

So far it had handicapped me a little, fighting with
a girl. I hadn't been at my best. Now that was
changed. She was a little rat of a murderer. She had
tried to kill me. A black rage swept me and the most
beautiful thing in the world just then was getting my
hands on her neck and splitting her scabby head
open on a rock. She would have liked to run from
the broken window now, but I went for her with
a rush. In a minute we were rolling in the trail,
clinching and gouging, panting and punching, and
tearing clothes.

I got her hair in both my hands and pounded her
head on the ground.

" You dirty bugger, you! " she screamed, and twisting, bit my hand to the bone.

From far away I had heard people call and now I was aware of spectators around us. They encouraged first one, then the other, yelling with Brewery Gulch delight at every scratch and blow. The girl could use her claws and teeth like a tiger cat, spitting in my face whenever she could do no more. But her tongue was the worst of her. She screamed curses, abuse, and filth on me I had never heard before.

Soon I was conscious of a warning buzz. The girl must have known what was coming and fought to get away, but I held on like a pair of nippers till I felt her jerked out of my grip as if I were straw. Looking up I saw a giant woman in an old skirt and striped, red, flying wrapper. Her face was like a stove casting. Loose iron-gray hair flung around it, and she had cheeks pink as a girl's.

" Ye Irish slut! " she roared, shaking her. " Heave a rock at my window light, will ye? "

" Let me have her! I'll tend to her! " I howled, jumping up.

" Ye will? " she jeered. " It's good I coom to pick 'er off your back or she'd a killed ye."

" I'd a licked her if you hadn't stopped me! " I bawled.

" It wasn't me broke it! " the girl screamed. " It was him."

" Him! " the Cornishwoman set her down hard and her eyes flamed as she came for me.

The second she was free the girl fled, and I at her heels. When she legged it downhill, I legged it

down, too, on a trail so steep I had to lean backward
to keep from falling. When she raced up the lower
street, I raced after her, past a buggy and a faded
house with a fancy wooden railing, into an alley-
way and over a fence and up a sandy arroyo with only
a trickle of water coming down, then up the side
of the gulch again till my chest pounded, by a red
wagon shed and around behind an empty, unpainted
house black as my father's on Cat Creek. Here she
tumbled to the ground to blow and I was so spent I
forgot everything except to throw myself down, too.
But I put some low cactus between us.

Where we were I didn't know except that it must
still be in Brewery Gulch. I could hear a distant blacksmith sharpening miners' steel. Whang,
whang, whang, he hammered. I could see houses
down below and up above through the sulphurous
red-brown smoke from the smelter.

The girl lifted her face above the cactus.

"You don't know nothing around here! " she
bragged. " I know everything."

"Everything about drunks? " I derided her.

" Sure," she said. " I know Mrs. Gavan and she's
a drunk. Her man don't dare give her money. He
has to buy even the flour himself and lock it up
when he goes to work or she'd sell it for liquor. That's
her walking down there now. You can tell it the way
she goes from side to side."

Far down on the street below I could make out
a small, dark-dressed woman hurrying along the
gulch, but it was a Mexican woman with a black
shawl over her head, and she walked a very straight
line.

" I know everybody in the gulch," the girl boasted.
" You see that man smoking up on his steps? I know
him. I know him good. That's Matt Kushto. He's
a Hunky. When he goes to church, he don't sit
down. He just stands and folds his arms like they
do in the old country. He got a prize for single-jacking once. He's on the graveyard shift."

I didn't know what single-jacking or the graveyard
shift were so I kept scornfully still.

" I bet you don't know who lives in that nice-
painted house. Mormons live there. They dance at
the Mormon church every Saturday night. He
wanted to bring a young wife home, but Mrs. Eberly
said she wouldn't have another woman sleeping in
a bed she saved for."

" I'm not scared of Mormons," I said.

" No, but you're scared to sleep in that house
down there with a tin roof on! Drapers lived in there
once. He poisoned his whole family with laudanum.
They're all buried in one grave. I can show you the
cemetery from here."

" I don't see any cemetery," I said.

" Can you see that woman sitting up on her
porch? "

" I can see three women up on their porch."

" I can see four — maybe five. But only one fat
one. That's Mrs. Farlaquatti. That's her boarding
house. She's rich. She owns six houses. Or seven.
She used to carry an umbrella when she went downtown. One time she took my mom along. My mom
liked something in the store, but she had no money
to buy it. When they got home, Mrs. Farlaquatti
gave it to her. She had it in the umbrella."

" That's stealing," I said.

" My mom didn't steal it. I'll knock you down if you say so."

I rolled over.

" I'll say it if I want to. But I don't want to. I never saw your mom."

" No, but I seen yours."

" She's not my mother." I got up suddenly. " I'm going home."

" Mrs. O'Dell'll get you! "

" I didn't bust her window," I said, starting away.

" I'm not scared of that big-footed, Cousin-Jack bastard! " the girl boasted, coming quickly after. She stopped at the black, unpainted house. " But I'm scared to go in here. Bedbugs'll drop on you. They'll suck your blood." She stuck her nose through a wide crack. " You can smell 'em."

" I don't smell anything," I scorned, trying it.

We stood each with a nose in a different crack, one eye straining around, trying to pierce the dimness within. I could hear her voice coming from that dark interior but I couldn't see anything.

" Old Jones built this house for a woman. He never seen her except her picture. She lived down South. They only could talk by letters. They were going to get married in it. Then she broke it off. She said she wouldn't live in it. It didn't have no bay window."

When I went on, the girl again took the lead. She showed the shortest way back to O.K. Trail. I could see scattered men and women still standing high up on their steps, but the girl only stopped once, to mimic some calling umbrella-mender down

in the gulch. Suddenly a man with a long nose ran
out behind us, and the Cornishwoman charged us
from a shed. We had no place to run except a blind
side gulch and they soon had us just as I saw Tacey's tall feather approaching up the hill. She had
been downtown and carried a package, probably of
cloth, in her hand. Already at the Pythian Castle she
must have seen the little crowd that had collected
around us, but made no hurry. Her walk had that
certain stiff quality again now that she was alone,
with one hand swinging too much. But when she
came closer and saw me held in the giant woman's
paw, my shirt bloody and torn to ribbons, all
that stopped. She had on her best tailored suit
and now that suit whipped toward us, her eyes very
green.

" What's the matter, Nugget? " she demanded in
a low voice.

Before I could answer, the Cornishwoman filled
her great barrel of a chest righteously.

" They were fighting like cat and dog, ma'am. Ye
can thank me for cooming and pulling them off
each other."

Tacey's eyes rested on the giant woman coldly,
then returned to me.

" Who's this kid you were fighting with? "

" She lives up there." I pointed with my chin.

" It's Seely Dowden," several called. " Your neighbor lass."

Tacey turned to the girl, who stood gazing at the
stylish, fur-trimmed suit with an expression I
couldn't fathom.

" What were you fighting about, Seely? "

The girl's eyes withdrew behind slits. She would say nothing. Tacey turned again to me.

"What did she do to you?"

"Nothing," I said and a big laugh went up at the sight of me.

"She's bad as they coom, ma'am," the Cornish-woman boomed. "Her own mother killed herself and left a small baby. Her father's black Irish as the devil cooks them. Ye want to watch what ye say to 'er or she'll tear them fine clothes off yer back and half yer skin besides."

The crowd laughed again. I had noticed at the White Palace Tacey's superiority to those she considered less than herself. She had no atom of fear for the women at the house, treated them hard and even imperiously. Now she just lifted her head and looked at these Brewery Gulch people and the laugh died on the air. Even the formidable Cornishwoman seemed to shrink.

"How aboot my window light, ma'am? He broke it, she says, and it cost me six shilling."

"If Nugget broke it, I'll pay for it," Tacey said shortly.

"Aye, but when?" the Cornishwoman begged. "A promise keeps no cold out the 'ouse. I can't stand the draft. I'm no the woman I once was. Not since I spaded forty acres. Spaded, mind ye. That's what done me up."

"You look well and strong," Tacey said coolly.

"Aye, I was that once. My first hoosband put me down in his prospect hole to dig. I dug so lively, ma'am, it near broke his back at the windlass pulling it up. He had to give it up and go down in the

hole digging hisself. Well, I had so much time to me-
self at the windlass, I cut down logs and dragged
'em in for a new 'ouse and barn."

Tacey did not say anything. The woman went on.

" He was the good hoosband, ma'am. So good the
Lord took him. And my next hoosband was so bad
the devil took him. Now I got a third and he's so
worthless, ma'am, the Lord nor devil'll have him
neither one."

The crowd tittered and I saw the man who had
helped to catch us slipping away.

" I'll pay you fifty cents for the window," Tacey
offered crisply.

The Cornishwoman suddenly let go of my hand
and I sprang up five or six of our steps.

" You're a fool if you pay her! " I yelled down.
" That girl's the one that broke it."

" Then Seely can pay me later," Tacey answered.

I stood there incredulous at her interest in the girl
and cold with jealousy. The girl shot me a venom-
ous look of triumph.

" Yes, I can wait here all day with my throat
cut! " I bawled.

" You're not hurt! " the girl jeered. " Pete Muz-
zo's guts lay in the street when he was stabbed. The
doctor had to sew them back along with a lot of
dried horse dung."

" That's enough, Seely! " Tacey said quietly. She
paid the Cornishwoman, then regarded the girl with
that inexplicable green eye of hers. " Do you want
to come with Nugget and me? " she asked, and held
out a gloved hand.

But the girl wouldn't take it.

" Take the lady's 'and or I'll crack ye! " the Cornishwoman roared.

The girl obeyed but her mouth drew down hard. Hand in hand she and Tacey moved toward our steps.

" I have something up at the house to show you," Tacey promised.

The girl didn't answer. She kept her head down till they reached our lowermost step. Suddenly she snatched her hand free and ran for her own steps only a few yards away. Without pausing once or looking back, her legs flew up the long flight. She popped into her house and violently slammed the door. You could hear it all over the gulch.

The Youngblood Hill people grinned with delight.

" I could 'ave told ye," the Cornishwoman said. " 'Er old man tried to tame her once. 'E stood on her neck. 'E might as well stood on a powder stick all the good it did, ma'am."

I thought it served Tacey right as she came up the steps alone. As she unlocked the door I saw her stop a moment to listen to a baby crying in the Dowden cabin next door.

Chapter 6

THE WHEEL

WE were out on the steps when the news came.

By night it often froze in Bisbee and any time during the winter day you could find the chill still hiding in the shadows. But around noon when the southwestern sun poured down from overhead, it filled the gulch like a great rocky chamber and then for a while it was almost like summer. You could even sit out in your shirt-sleeves.

Sunny mornings Tacey would come out. She'd twist a little at first, even with the colored afghan around her shoulders. Any moment I'd expect her to jump up and go back in the house. Then as the sun warmed through, she would look around. Our porch was like a high seat in the balcony of a vast theater. Brewery Gulch was the stage, with painted wings and scenery and always actors moving across it. It was a show you never tired of seeing. Day after day I saw the same men off their shifts watching from the same places.

But Tacey seldom stayed out long. After a while she would hurry back in the house. What she hurried for I don't think she knew herself except that something in her went too fast. Once Gaye demanded what she wanted to get up at nine o'clock of a morning for, and she cut him off that if she lay in bed another minute she'd go out of her mind. I slept on the bunk in the little front room and was glad to hear her up. I knew that in a relatively few minutes her breakfast and mine, such as it was, would be standing hot on the pine table. You'd think, Gaye said, I was a grown man with a shift at the mines and my pay to be docked if I was late. I never even had a dish to dry. She had them washed, dried, put away, and the dishpan emptied over the cliff before I could lug a bucket of fresh water up from the hydrant down by the trail.

I think they got washed and dried all too soon even for her and that she tried to hold them back without success. The dishes done, she'd make the two empty bunks. She was surprisingly competent at housework. A fling at one end of a sheet or blanket and the far corner would drop accurately into its proper place. Kitchen, front room, and porch she swept each morning whether they needed it or not. Very soon everything in the little house was done and something desperate showed in her eye as it looked around for more to do and nothing there.

Afternoons she walked downtown. Sometimes it was for one or two small groceries, sometimes to the post office to see if her latest pattern had come,

sometimes to the company store or the Fair for
thread, buttons, or cloth. I even heard her ask for
pins with certain, special-colored heads. She liked
to have me along. Sometimes we'd walk over the
hills instead, among the acorn trees to Walnut
Springs or Dixie or Dubaker Canyons or perhaps to
a place she had never seen before. Tacey was a good
walker. Her legs and arms liked action and she
would talk freely when she got warmed up. But evenings after Gaye had gone to work at the Sports
Club Saloon, she kept her thoughts to herself over
her sewing. Her hands were very fast and clever.
With a needle, thread, and pair of scissors they could
make most anything.

She had one curious trick of having Gaye or me
tickle her legs. It seemed perfectly natural to me as
a boy, just something a girl was partial to. She would
lean back and almost close her eyes while one of us
ran the tips of his fingers lazily up and down the
curve of her calf and ankle. We couldn't do it too
long for her. Tacey's figure was slight and the strong
way her legs filled her stockings surprised me. Just
a glance at them told that they could kick plenty
high and hard. They always looked longer than I
expected. I can still see them, powerful in their black
lisle hose, and feel the peculiar sensation they gave
me.

Between eight and nine o'clock of an evening I
was sent to bed. Tacey would take her lamp and
sewing into the kitchen. She closed the door but in
a short time I could smell very plainly the drift of
cigarette smoke in the dark room. Sometimes I noticed it again after she was in bed. About ten o'clock,

if I was awake, I could hear her raise her sash high
enough to put a spool underneath. Then there was
no sound until Gaye came in. His arrival home at
that early hour was usually the top mark of the day.
If he didn't tell a thing then, he never would.
Through my disturbed sleep I would hear the high-
lights of the night's work, including any news or
choice story he had heard.

Most of Gaye's stories were more or less shady.
His funniest was about the foreigner he had seen,
running, jumping up and down, and pounding on
a certain, well-known outside door that happened to
be locked while the train stopped at Bisbee. But it
took Gaye to tell that one in all its detail, and I
won't try. He had a dry, unhurried way with a story,
his face puckered up to put you in the proper mood
and give you a taste of what was to come. Even in
the darkness of my room I could see his face when
he was talking. The other story was of the time Mike
Crowley and his friends made the rounds in a hack
till they came to Frank Drumm's saloon in Lowell.
It was just getting daylight and the saloon was deserted except for Drumm's cross bulldog. Every time
they tried the door, which was open, the dog nearly
tore down the place. The others wanted to go back
to Bisbee but Mike said he wouldn't go back without
a drink. He was a little heavy-set man with a jag on.
He said he'd fix that bulldog. He just took off his
pants, bent over, and backed into the saloon and
Gaye said that surprised bulldog came running out
like a bat out of hell. Tacey had a curious blaring
laugh that didn't sound like her at all. It was usually
over at once as if she had forgotten herself and let

out something she hadn't meant to. To my surprise, she shouted with unstifled laughter at the bulldog story.

As I said before, Tacey and I were sitting out on the steps. Gaye was still sleeping. Seely must have seen Tacey and me, but there was never a sign of her. Ever since she owed Tacey for the broken window, she had kept away from us as the very devil. Once when I had come out suddenly I had caught her sitting with the baby on the narrow and dangerous ledge between the two houses. But before I had a good look, she had snatched it up and made tracks back to her cabin with the live squirming bundle half as big as she was, and the trailing blanket trying to trip her at every step.

About eleven o'clock we saw a miner coming up O.K. Street with his dinner bucket flashing signals in the sun. The whole gulch knew that the daylight shift didn't come out until eleven and we soon saw women hurrying down more than one flight of steps, pulling shawls over their heads or shoulders. By the time he reached the trail, a dozen surrounded him. Some of these went down with him to Donahue's whitewashed house next to the Cornishwoman's, some stayed talking in the trail. Now and then they would look up our way. Presently three women appeared resolutely from the whitewashed house and started to climb the Dowden steps.

The Cornishwoman was among them and halfway up she called to Tacey as she climbed.

" Ye ever get paid back for that windy light, ma'am? "

" I will be, Mrs. Odell," Tacey answered coolly.

You could tell she didn't care to discuss the matter
in front of Brewery Gulch.

"If you don't 'ave it now, ye never will," the Cornishwoman came back. "Her old man got blowed
to hell today."

I saw Tacey glance quickly at the Dowden house.
The front door stood open to the sun but there was
no sign that anyone was about.

"Anything wrong?" At the green house beyond
the Dowden place a woman had come out on her
high porch.

"Accident at the Czar shaft!" the Cornishwoman bawled back. "One o' Tim Dowden's shots
didn't go off with the rest."

"Is he hurt?"

"They said he counted twelve before he went
back. But he must 'ave drilled thirteen. He never
could count anyway."

"Is he hurt bad?"

"Sommat. It blowed the top of his head off."

"Why, his woman ain't dead a year yet," the
woman at the green house called, bending over her
railing.

"Well, she's saved the trouble o' burying him,"
the Cornishwoman answered complacently.

Over at the open door I had a moment's glimpse
of a child's white face. Then the door slammed. At
the sound, the Cornishwoman looked up indig-
nantly. When they got to the little bare porch, they
found the door locked.

"Open up, Seely!" the Cornishwoman wheedled.

"Go on down!" we could hear Seely's muffled
shout. "I didn't ask you up."

" I got some news for ye," the Cornishwoman said piously, her mouth close to the crack at the doorjamb.

" It's a lie! " Seely shouted. " You bastards made it up."

" Open this door! " the Cornishwoman warned, rattling the latch in her huge hand.

" I got the axe! " Seely screamed. " You better go down, you big-footed son-of-a-bitch! "

Tacey rose sharply from her step. For a moment I thought she was going away from that kind of language. When I looked again, she was moving swiftly across the narrow, dangerous ledge between the two houses. She went around the rear of the house and I ran after.

At the sound of her back door opening, Seely came charging back, her face distorted, in her hands a rusty old axe. Then she saw who it was. Her face, already twisted with fury, screwed up with sudden grief.

" Oh, ma'am! " she sobbed, and buried herself in Tacey's skirt.

For a minute Tacey let her cry or choke or whatever it was she was doing. It sounded like merely trying to draw her breath through the tears and spit in her throat. All the time the Cornishwoman pounded and threatened from the front door. You could see she wouldn't be made a fool of in front of the other women and the watchers below. But when Tacey opened the door the high red bluster melted on her face like butter.

For ten or fifteen minutes Tacey had to talk and listen. She stood in the middle of the doorway so

firmly that none of them dared push through. But
they looked in around her and left no detail of the
accident untold. They said the corpse would have
to wear a cap in the coffin. The men would be bringing him up after a while. He hadn't two bits in his
pocket when they found him. The sheriff was down
in the Czar shaft now taking depositions. The men
would blast out a grave.

"He won't keep much over tomorrow," one of
the women advised.

"He might," the Cornishwoman declared toler-
antly, " if Doc Mitchell gutted him like he did that
consumptive for back east."

The third woman threw her head back in a short
laugh.

"He gave a dollar to a nigger woman," she told
Tacey. "She was supposed to bury the insides. She
threw them out in the alley and the hogs dragged
them all over town."

While they talked, the child, Seely, stood with
her face hard and twisted, watching them from cruel
eyes, her lips moving as if any moment a torrent of
black abuse would pour forth. The minute they left,
she ran in to the crying baby.

I had wondered what the other room in the cabin
looked like, but one look through the open door
was enough. Our house along Cat Creek had been
bad but nothing like this. It was as if a tornado had
struck it months ago and nothing done since. In the
midst of the disorder lay the crusty baby, pale even
when it screamed, its nose running and its unwashed
dress stained with vile-colored drool.

Tacey steelly avoided my eyes.

"Go on outside, Nugget. Tell me if you see any-body coming. When Gaye gets up, tell him he can get his own dinner today."

Out on the steps Seely hurried by me down and back, once with a pitcher for milk and once for a bucket of hydrant water. She paid me ut-terly no attention. She and Tacey might have been members of some secret order from which I was barred. By now, I noticed, the baby had stopped crying.

I didn't mind being outside, where even the tin cans looked orderly. But I hated to tell Gaye he had to get his own dinner. Tomorrow he was dealing his first faro bank, on Smiley Bursum's night off. I thought Tacey shouldn't make a banker get his own dinner — even if he was a banker only for one night. Anyway it was at the Empire where great men like Cap Brown and Senator Watrous drank and gam-bled, hidden behind luxurious gray window curtains embroidered with a big E.

Gaye gave me a funny stare when I told him.

"What's she doing over there?"

Soon afterward I heard his feet jog rapidly down the steps. It was as if he wanted to get away. He threw an uneasy look toward the Dowden cabin as he went.

Within the hour I called to Tacey that they were bringing Seely's father up the gulch. I could see four men instead of two at the covered stretcher. It was a slow procession but no silent or solemn one. At the bottom of the Dowden steps I expected them to sub-side but they had let down the stretcher and lifted back the tarpaulin in too many saloons on the way.

Also, Tim Dowden had been a big man and the
steps were steep.

"Now we got to climb the damn mountain."

"Where's the cage?"

"Take it easy, Mac. Tim left no whisky up there
for you."

"No and it's all turned to lead in the old devil."

"You workin' or ridin', Donahue?"

"I'm lifting, you lousy bastards. What are you
doing?"

"Why don't we keep the corpse at Donahue's?"

"A pity it ain't Donyhue hisself. Look at the little
ways we'd have to drag him."

"Like hell! I'm moving to the top of Mule Mountain before I kick off. Then you bastards can work
on me till your tongues hang out."

"Aye, maybe we'll pick you up in a bucket."

"Hist your end, Mac! He's got no top of the head
to stand on."

"Why didn't we move the damned house down!"

The farther up they struggled, the more the steps
shook under the five men and the harder the male-
dictions flew. It all seemed fitting enough when I
remembered the times I had heard Tim Dowden in
the flesh coming up these same steps. If the hour
was late, he was usually drunk, singing a scurrilous
song about an old woman. It would have put him in
jail had he sung it down near the Douglas or Watrous mansions. Along O.K. Street and Trail nobody
bothered him, and his headway was steady enough.
When he came to the bottom of the steps you could
tell by the loud interjections that someone was there.
Doubtless the child, Seely, had heard his signals and

was waiting to pilot him up the steep flight. His
progress from this point was a succession of stops
and starts, of loud curses, protests, and interjections. Lying in my bunk in the darkness, I could see
clearly in my mind the long procession of missteps
and pauses, of slips and swayings and narrow es-
capes till the slam of the door announced he had
made it and was safe for a while between four walls.

The way Tacey had stood off the Cornishwoman
I thought she meant to let no one in the house until
after the funeral. But it must have been for a different reason. When she called me over for supper, I
hardly knew the place. Even Seely had a clean dress
on. Her face looked scrubbed and her hair was aston-
ishingly up in curlers. Tacey moved about as if nothing had happened, but I saw Seely's eyes keep returning to a dim object between two front-room
chairs. When Tacey moved, the child's eyes flew
back to her. And when Tacey went out in back,
Seely ran after, claiming she had to go, too.

Tacey came home but once that night and then
only for a minute. I had stayed in our kitchen. From
where I sat I could see the lighted windows of the
Dowden house and hear the voices of many men
and women. I could see Tacey, too, when she passed
the window. She was as I hadn't seen her since the
White Palace. Slow, cool, watchful, and very intense, she carried herself as if this was her element
and she was in charge. When men held a bottle to
the mouth of a six-year-old sitting on the kitchen
table, she snatched it away and quickly sobered the
uproarious laughter.

I was in bed when someone opened our front door.

" Who's that? " I asked, sitting up.

" It's me," Tacey's voice came swiftly. " Put these under your covers. They've had too much already. No woman's going to lose her skirt at this wake if I can help it." I heard the clink of jugs or heavy bottles at my feet and felt them tucked under the blankets.

Gaye slept right through the funeral. I sat on our little porch in the sun. Looking down into the gulf, it didn't seem as if anybody was dead. The neighboring houses stood as always. The brown smelter smoke hung everywhere and the white clouds sailed above it like ships. Down in Mrs. Janey's yard the tamarisks looked fresh and green. Kids too small for school ran up and down playing and yelling. But when you looked at the Dowden house you saw dresses sticking out of every door and window. And the words of the preacher that drifted out chilled me through.

The men sat in a long file down the steps, smoking, warming themselves in the sun. Their talk drifted up to where I sat. It was talk of the mines, of their bosses, of Butte and Alaska, of China Dot, the white consort of Lee Ginn, and of the big time you could have doing jury duty at Tombstone. Their only concessions to the funeral were their low tones and, when the service was over, a word about the corpse.

" Well, I done what Tim told me," Mac McGhee said.

The others stayed silent, a little uncomfortable. Mac went on:

" He said: ' Don't let anybody bury me alive. Hold a bottle to my nose. If I ain't dead, I'll sit up right now.' "

Nobody said anything for a little.

" He didn't sit up, did he? "

" No," Mac said soberly, reaching for a chew.

A few were coming slowly out of the house now. The preacher stood on the porch and beckoned. Some of the men rose and went up, pulling on their white gloves to show they were the pallbearers. In their strong hands the long box tacked outside with black cloth moved out of the door level enough. But soon it slanted deeply down as if it couldn't wait for the ground. I saw Seely moving clumsily behind it. Tacey came with her as far as the top of the steps, whispered something, and pushed her on alone. The child went unwillingly, bitterly, her dry hard eyes blinking in the sunlight. But when Mrs. Hannin, her other neighbor, pushed up beside her and tried to take her hand, Seely shook her off angrily and stalked down after the coffin alone.

I was soon to know, if I didn't already, the women who followed — Mrs. Farlaquatti, the fat boarding-house keeper; a bright little Cornishwoman, Mrs. Axtell, whose husband was foreman of the Czar shaft; and the other Cornishwoman, Mrs. O'Dell; Mrs. Gavan, the drunkard, sober and shabby; the Mormon's wife, Mrs. Eberly; the red-haired, sharp-voiced Swede, Mrs. Holmquist; Mrs. Kelly, the " widow " of an absent prospector; the woman who kept the chickens, Mrs. Capp; and Mrs. McGhee

who, people said, was really still Mrs. Shay. Strap-
ping Slovak and Polack women walked behind, with
bright aprons over their great bellies, giantesses beside the little old Mexican women, who turned their
black-shawled heads this way and that like small,
wrinkled nuns.

Nearly everybody walked to the cemetery to see
the grave. Already when we got there a small crowd
stood around it, gazing down its flaked sides. The
men on Tim Dowden's shift had drilled it out of
solid rock as befitted a hard rock miner. All through
the burial service people kept pushing through to
crane their necks over the rocky hole. But either the
drillers or the cabinetmaker had made a miscalcu-
lation. When they lowered the coffin, it wouldn't
go down all the way at one end. Mike Donahue, one
of the pallbearers, jumped in the hole and stumped
on the box. Still it wouldn't go quite down.

" He never gets out of that! " Matt Kushto said,
appraising the walls expertly.

" Think of that drunken devil," the Morman
woman whispered to Mrs. Axtell, " in a sepulchre
like our Lord's."

When I got back to the house, Gaye was up and
dressed. He gave me a glum look.

" She still over there? "

I nodded. He sat at the kitchen table practicing
for Smiley Bursom's shift. He had borrowed an old
faro layout, complete with box and shuffling cloth
from Dappa Duke. The ancient card faces painted
on the layout were doubtless faded and worn but to
my boyish eyes they glowed like a church's stained-
glass windows. He shuffled the deck skillfully, not

half to half as the pikers did, which left telltale counters, but a third to two-thirds. Then he started drawing the cards one by one from the battered old silver box. As he drew, I could see his lips move and knew he was making bets for imaginary customers. Deftly he slapped stacks of chips — we always called them checks — on certain cards of the layout. He was still at it when they came in, Tacey ahead with her bundle, Seely just behind her. Gaye must have heard, but his back was toward them and I think he thought it was only Tacey. Now he'd show her the same neglect she showed him and incidentally what he could do at faro. They stood perfectly still, watching while he finished his game.

I could see that the idea of Tacey as a spectator stimulated him more than I had done. Those square brown hands of his literally flew. His pay-off of imaginary bets — so many white chips here and blue and red there, all with an instant sweep of his hand out of which the three colors magically came without counting or mistake — was a beautiful thing to see. When he spoke in his calm way: "Last turn! Four to one if you call it!" I saw Seely give a sharp look of delight at Tacey as if he had called it to her.

He went through it all without a hitch. You could tell it had pleased him, and his pleasure came out in his hands. Lifting the cut deck they shuffled it in mid air so fast the cards were a blur in his fingers. This was only for show-off. At work he wouldn't think of shuffling except on the table. Then came the final touch of his prowess. He took a red stack of chips and a white one and drew his hand over them. Now it was only one tall stack mixed red and white like peppermint candy. He cut the stack and did it again. The third time they were back to solid colors again.

" Ain't he wonderful! " Seely said to Tacey out loud.

Gaye turned instantly and saw her. He got up annoyed, his face freezing as he saw the blanketed bundle in Tacey's arms. She had a strange, softly triumphant look on her face.

" Somebody here to see you, Gaye! " she said, folding back the blanket and showing a face like a little old man with his thumb in his mouth.

The girls at the White Palace had said you couldn't tell from Gaye's face whether the house was winning or going broke. They said the weepers made no more dent on him than a duck quacking. I wondered what they'd have thought of him now.

" Somebody coming for those kids tonight? " he asked her.

" Not if I can help it! " she told him quickly.

" Where's their relations? " Fear was all over him.

" They don't have any."

" Look here, Tacey! " I had never seen his face so funny-colored and thick at the jaws.

" Say it! " she cried, her eyes green now and ready to fight.

" You think you're bringing luck in this house? "

" What do you want me to do? Throw them over the cliff? "

Like always when they got so far toward a fight, his nature came over him like a coat of flat paint. He turned to the table, gripped Seely's wrist till she dropped a fistful of chips, then started sorting and packing them. The deck went in the silver box, and the layout folded up like a napkin. Afterward he put on his tie and before his coat, his waistcoat. Last his hat, not back on the side of his head, but clamped down in front, and out he went, not a word between his teeth.

I was all on his side. I didn't like the Dowdens coming to live at our house, either. Besides I knew that luck was his business. Of course you had to be smarter than the pikers. But luck was the main thing. I had heard Gaye say it myself. If good luck turned up, play. If bad luck showed in a row, stop. Don't play that night at all. If you want to be lucky, be with lucky people. And the other way around, for bad luck was catching as smallpox. Too bad what had happened to Tim Dowden and his woman, but what did Tacey want to turn their bad streak on us for?

I lay in bed that night wondering what, if anything, might happen. Tacey was the one who had brought the bad luck to the house. It would probably hit her first. Besides, she had Seely sleeping with her in her bunk. But I was exposed, too. Timmy, the baby, slept in a drawer not eight feet from my head. There wasn't room in the sleeping-room for all and Tacey had kept her door open. Gaye would be mad to find how everything was when he got in.

It was still dark when he came. I couldn't see much of him, just the glow of his cigar crossing the room. I lay there expecting the fuss to be picked up where they had left off. I could hear a sinister clinking on the built-in bureau before he undressed and crawled into his bunk. Then a long silence. Not a word.

I knew Tacey wasn't sleeping. She could never sleep with him coming in. Every nerve would tingle. She would have to flare out. She couldn't stand keeping quiet. But it turned out to be Gaye who couldn't stand it.

" Tacey! " he said in a low voice.

" Shh! " she hissed from her bed.

" Thought you'd want to hear this," he went on. " Smiley's going to Tombstone for good. The floor-man gave me his shift."

Incredulous silence. Gaye a regular faro banker at the Empire!

" So they didn't bring you such bad luck! " Tacey whispered sarcastically.

" Nope," Gaye said, matter-of-fact. " After I knew it, I bucked the wheel a little at the Sports Club. Took a hundred and sixty from the house. It's there for you on your bureau."

" Sh! " Tacey hissed at him vigorously. " You'll wake up the kids."

Chapter 7

SLOW SUNSHINE

I BLAMED Tacey for it. Not that I liked Seely, but she had been with us only two or three days and already Tacey was trying to make a lady of her. I remember Choppo Garcia's three burros had fetched us a jag of wood that day. Had there been any kind of path up the cliff, they'd have balanced their great, rounded packs right up to our back door. But there wasn't any path and Choppo had taken off the ropes and dumped the wood right on O.K. Trail. Seely and I had to pile it on our lower steps so people could get by. The pile rolled and caught her finger and she ripped out a long oath furbished up with two or three unprintable parts and functions of the anatomy. As I say, we were down at the bottom of the steps, but a whirlwind of skirts and heel clicks blew somewhere above us.

" Seely! " an angry, imperious voice called. When

we looked up, there was Tacey on the porch and something terrible in her face.

" Damn it to hell! " Seely muttered. " What did I do now? "

" You'll get the devil! " I promised.

Seely raised her face.

" I didn't mean to say that, ma'am," she whined.

" Come up here! " Tacey ordered.

What happened in the secrecy of the house I don't know because I had to stay down and finish piling up the wood myself. But I recall that when I carried up my first armful I met Seely coming down, and her face was black and rebellious as thunder.

That was one day. Next afternoon when I came in I knew at once that there was something strange in the house. I found it on Tacey's counterpane, a small pile of newly bought cloth, gray tumbled with vivid red. It was the red that I had smelled, strong with dyes as the red copper water in the board tanks at the Lowell shaft. By evening Tacey had the cloth sheared and basted, the gray hanging on me and the bright red plaid on Seely, with gaping holes for arms and wonder in me that these fantastic shapes would ever make a finished garment. You would have thought she would have taken one of us first and finished before going to the next but, we had to stand there together like brother and sister who would howl if one got an inch ahead of the other, while she put us through our fittings, going around us on her knees with her mouth full of pins, telling us to stand straight or keep quiet. All the time those slight-looking white hands of hers swiftly folded this and pinned that and tucked here and jerked there.

Her eyes were all on her work. I felt they scarcely saw the real us at all. Her knees kept going around us two or three times each until she was satisfied.

My gray had looped diagonals of darker gray running down sidewise as if the field of cloth had been plowed kitty-cornered. Seely's plaid had squares of dark red and squares of light red and squares of black, all with fine yellow lines, far apart, cutting them. Tacey said light gray was very becoming to me but I knew she said it to offset the way the red plaid brought Seely out. She looked absolutely stunning in it, the red against the black of her hair and eyes dark from her eyebrows. Seely must have known by some instinct of her sex how she looked. There was no looking-glass in the cabin large enough to tell her, yet she went around in a kind of hypnotic spell, holding the skirt up in front of her as if it was threaded with gold. You could see that the dress had bought her, body and soul.

Sunday evening Tacey went over us a last time, nipping off threads, trying buttons in buttonholes, then off with our new clothes and out with them to the kitchen to go under the flatiron.

" You can go to bed now," she told us. " Tomorrow you go to school."

" School? " I swallowed incredulously.

" Don't you want to be somebody? " Tacey flashed at me.

" I don't even know where to go," I stammered defiantly, but Seely didn't fight or object.

" I'll show him, ma'am," she said, meeker and sweeter than I had ever heard her, and I saw her eyes fastened on her red plaid dress.

I knew better than say any more at the time, and never a word next morning when Tacey sent us off together, the gray and the red, but something ate into me bitter as copper water. I could see now that Tacey didn't need me around the house any more. She had others for pastime and company.

" You turn up here! " down in the gulch Seely said to me in her new, stilted, fine-dress manner.

" You turn down here! " I mocked her and ran around by Main Street, climbing School Hill by myself as the last bell rang. I needed no girl to take me to school. Besides, coming from eastern Kansas to this Western mining camp, I had no intention of starting in Seely's Secondary.

That Bisbee Secondary! For years Tacey hoarded a picture of it, a big picture on curved gray cardboard with all the kids of the room who had come that day standing crowded together on the steps. Today your finger might go over it row by row and call out the Irish, Cornish, Slovak, Polish, Italian, Mexican, and Swedish faces. But you could never pick out which was Seely standing in the center in her plaid dress or me on the end with a spreading white collar and a store-tied bow. Miss Pritchard with the biggest girls beside her stood back in the doorway. How many times have I run through that scarred doorway! You came first into the hall that some called the cloakroom, with the girls' capes on one side and the boys caps on the other. Then it was only a step to the schoolroom, with its unforgettable smell of chalk dust and spit-wiped slates. Your shoes, if you didn't lift them, would pick up long floor splinters, and on certain desks besides initials was carved the obscene diamond, even at that tender age. To me the room always had a mellow, faded sunny look, the picture of George Washington on the wall, the crossed flags, even the stiff inverted pear bosom of Miss Pritchard standing at the painted board blackboard, her pointer heavy as a billiard cue in front of her and behind her the sky-green copper ore some kids had brought for her desk.

All day I avoided a mincing Seely in her fine dress, though I could feel her eyes on me reproachfully. I ran home by the cemetery for dinner and beat her back to school for the afternoon. At recess I stayed on the boys' side of the school grounds, watching them play chips. That's the game I would like to see them play again, sailing a saloon chip from a spinning top, and an expert hand it took. Steve Morrow was the champion at it, but red-headed Matt Mac-Cachy could beat him at big ring, where whenever your top knocked another from the ring, it was your top.

" You going home? " Seely asked me after school.

" No," I said and turned back on her and waited for her to go meekly down in her stilted new walk, careful of her red dress lest she get something on it. Then I started home around by the cemetery.

On the school grounds none of the boys had paid any more attention to me than Mrs. Wilson's red rooster, but when I got to the cemetery I saw five boys waiting on the dead grass. Just the lazy way they lay there, some on one side of the path, some on the other, signaled caution. None of them looked my way but beyond them I saw smaller kids sitting on tombstones like seats at a bullfight and expect-antly waiting. Now the boys on the grass were getting up carefully.

There was something about Bisbee men I had noticed from the first day we came. On the street even among friends they stood around tough and stiff-legged, their eyes dark and challenging. They stood like prizefighters flexed for a picture. You wouldn't believe they could hold it, but when you came by an hour later they stood there the same way. It was natural to them as breathing.

That's the way the five Secondary boys stood waiting for me in the cemetery now.

" Hi ya, kids? " I ventured.

" Who're you? " the littlest one challenged. Some of them gave him a push and he stepped out aside of me in the path. He came only a bit above my shoulder. He stood as close to me as he could and looked me up and down. " I can lick the pants off you! " he said.

" Go home to your mom," I told him and started on.

For a minute we moved slowly, stiff-legged and shoulder to shoulder, along the path. We were like a pair of small stepping dogs, rigid from nose to tail, looking ahead but watching the other, waiting for him to snap first.

" Put a chip on him! " Steve Morrow called.

I thought they meant me, but they picked up a twig and set it on the shoulder of my little adversary.

" Knock it off! " he dared me, drawing back.

" I don't have to knock it off for you or anybody like you! " I answered just as hard as he, and kept on going.

"Put it on him, I said!" Steve Morrow called again.

I brushed it off the second they set it there. Before they could do it again, we came to a tombstone against the path and my small adversary had to go around it. That eased the tension and I seized the moment to walk faster.

But it was only for a minute. The others came running up around me.

"Where d'y think you're from?" Leo Killian asked me with contempt.

"School," I told him.

"School! He says school!" he jeered. "Where'd you come to Bisbee from?"

"Kansas," I said.

"Kan-zass!" those behind me yelled together and jerked my cap down so it stuck over my eyes.

I pulled it up hot and angered, but when I saw again how many there were and all waiting for me to start something, I pushed doggedly on.

"What's your name, Kan-zass?" one called behind me.

I made no answer, just kept putting one foot ahead of the other, slowly enough so it couldn't be called running.

"It's Nugget Oldaker," a little girl standing on a square tombstone called.

They howled an ugly rhyme with delight and at the top of their lungs, while the little girl on the tombstone stood there owl-faced, feasting, and never blinked an eye.

"Give him the third degree, Leo!" an Italian boy called.

"We'll see what he's got," the big Irish boy promised. "Then all you kids can spit on it."

I moved no faster but a slow, cold horror came up in me.

The cemetery is gone now and a park stands in its place. When I go back I marvel what a narrow little place it must have been, but it seemed a long way across it then. They were close and hard around me, and I could smell their breathing. First a push on one side, and when I turned, a push on the other. Had I had sense I would have kept going. But I would strike out in front and they would goose me from behind. Soon they had me losing my head, and not even a blow struck as yet. I could see a colored stream of dresses, a bright red plaid among them, flowing back up the hill to watch the fight. They gave me a sick feeling at my stomach.

When we came to the umbrella tree that used to stand in the cemetery, one of them pulled off my cap from behind.

"Fix it, Barney!" they yelled.

The boy that had it ran, turned his back, and fumbled with his clothing. I knew instantly what he was up to. I made a rush and he threw the cap up in the umbrella tree, where it stuck. That decided it. I could never go home and leave it behind me now. And if I climbed for it I was a fool. I would never get home anyway. Home was across Brewery Gulch and that was as far as Kansas. Let them kill me here in the cemetery, I thought, but the blood of the boy who tried to do that to my cap would be hot and sweet on my hands first.

He couldn't stand up to the murder in my rush,

and down he went, but I had no time to feed my
hate on him. I had to turn and meet the others.
Their fists had the feel of rocks on my head and face.
This was the chance they had been waiting for.
Through a growing numbness I went down, but as
I went I saw a red dress come charging.

" You dirty bastards, let my brother alone! " the
girl in it screamed, and I knew that, though it was me
they pounded, those fists had knocked the veneer
off of Seely Dowden.

They said in the gulch afterward that Patrick
Connelly, Born 1851, Died, 1892, had got in the
fight. Anyway Seely pushed his gravestone over us.
That's the only time I was glad to be on the bottom.
I never felt it but I heard a boy yell wildly with pain,
then most of us were on our feet again and Seely was
in it along with me, hitting, scratching, butting,
kicking, and crying out epithets that made the little
girls on the flat tombstone jump up and down. Steve
Morrow fell against the little metallic fence around
a child's grave, and when he lifted his head, blood
lay like red lightning over his half-Greek face.

" Kill the bastards! " Seely was squealing.
" Knock their lousy heads off."

Only three of the five were in the fight now and
Seely and I threw ourselves with triumphant ferocity
on the rest. The Italian boy ran. In a while there
was only the littlest boy left, his face streaked with
dirt and trying hard to get away. Seely held to him,
savagely jerking and ripping till she had him on the
ground and his corduroys pulled off and one of his
shoes with them.

" Give me my pants! " he howled, all the fight out

of him, standing there naked from knees to waist
and not a girl turning her head.

"I'll give 'em to you!" Seely panted, her head
forward and blood wicked over her eye. "When you
get down his cap."

"I didn't throw it up!" he bawled.

"Well, you'll get it down," Seely told him, "or
you go home with your backside sticking out."

Crying now that I felt shame for him, half blinded
with sand and tears, the barelegged boy climbed up
in the tree and shook down the cap. Seely's eyes
blazed.

"Don't you pick it up, Nugget. Let him hand it
to you himself."

"Come on," I told her. "Give him his old pants."

But Seely in anger waited till he was down.

"Here, then!" she told him. "Here are your dirty
old pants." And she threw them savagely up on the
tree where they hung. "Now you can climb up
again, you naked baboon!" Looking back from time
to time belligerently and triumphantly, she went
with me down the path.

By the time we reached O.K. Trail, however, she
had sobered, and so had I. We climbed the long
steps slowly and thoughtfully.

"Remember, we didn't do nothing!" she whispered to me. "They did the whole thing. They
jumped us from first to last. Me and you both. We
were just coming home together."

I didn't say anything, relieved that Tacey wouldn't
know that Seely had to help me. We went around
the back way. The kitchen was empty and we stayed
there quietly cleaning ourselves as best we could

until Tacey's voice called suspiciously. She was in the front room sewing, the baby propped up in my bunk.

She gave us a close, enigmatic look.

" So that's why you didn't come in."

" We didn't do anything, ma'am," Seely begged quickly. " They did it. They laid for us. That's how they do to a new kid like Nugget. They piled on us and drug us around. We couldn't do anything. They were bigger'n us. Intermediates, weren't they, Nugget? We never lifted a finger."

Tacey rose.

" Well, why didn't you? "

" You said about a lady, ma'am," Seely stammered.

" A lady doesn't let anybody do that to her! " Tacey blazed. " Look at your clothes." She lay down her sewing and got her hat and smart jacket with the fur. " Nugget, you stay here with Timmy. Seely can take me where those Intermediates live."

Seely gave me a foiled helpless look.

" Maybe some were Secondaries, ma'am," she said.

Tacey's green eyes seared us.

" Listen, you kids. Remember, you can't fool me. I've been through all this. If you were in a fight and need new clothes, I'll make them for you. But if you lie to me, I'll whip you."

" Yes, ma'am," Seely said with relief. " I guess we had to fight back a little. You got to be tough in Bisbee. Millie Aikin won't fight back and the boys lift her dress up all the way home."

" I'm not talking about your fighting back," Tacey

turned on her. " I'm talking about your lying."

" Yes, ma'am," Seely said, subdued.

" Now tell me what happened. And don't leave anything out."

I told the first part and Seely from then on. She told it reluctantly as if she didn't know how Tacey would take certain things. But when she came to Patrick Connelly's tombstone and how she had pushed it on the cursing Leo Killian, Tacey gave her unexpected blaring laugh.

Seely looked eager.

" If you want to hear some real swearing, ma'am — "

" I don't," Tacey cut her off.

" No, ma'am," Seely agreed soberly.

Chapter 8

THE FOUNTAIN

As regular as a mine boss's lady, Tacey went down to Main Street Saturday and bought her Sunday things. She liked to mingle with the crowd. Not that Brewery Gulch wasn't crowded. Every day at midnight or noon you couldn't walk down the lower end of the gulch except through hundreds of men. Miners off their shift sat packed along the edge of the boardwalks, or knotted themselves in the street and before saloon and rooming-hotel doors. Eighteen or twenty bar-rooms, counting both sides of the street, had thrown their keys away.

It would have been easier to leave the baby at home with one of us kids to mind it, but Tacey liked to have us with her, and especially the baby. She would sail along with a slow genteel air of security, her little brood about her, all of us taking turns carrying the baby. It was one chore Seely and I never minded. We knew Tacey's pocketbook had a dime for each of us when we reached the company store.

This had been going on for nearly two years, and our route today was the same. After Brewery Gulch, Main Street always seemed like a different world, the great mine offices set behind shade trees and the big Douglas house beside them. The company store stood right across the street, but first we had to pass the other stores, the Empire Saloon and the Watrous mansion with its " fountain." The latter was a rocky garden pool such as only the very rich those days could afford, with a lily pad or two and if the sun was right, the chance of seeing a large red and white goldfish swimming around. A small statue stood above it of a barefoot boy, blowing his pipe, and out of the pipe, when water was plentiful, a thin stream rose a few inches into the air and then fell or trickled down over the statue to the pool. At those rare times when the fountain was on, I have seen Seely stand gazing through the tall iron spikes, her head a little to one side, just content to stand there, a curious look on her tough young face.

Tacey, I noticed, watched the Watrous place, too, but with her it was the house rather than the fountain, and the hope, I think, of seeing someone go in or out. Going up on one side of the street and coming back on the other, her green eyes, fixed on the mansion through her veil, missed nothing. At Castle Rock it was our custom to turn around, but we didn't get that far today. A two-horse carriage came down the rocky bed of the canyon. The coachman was a fattish, owl-faced Mexican but the sun on the polished wheels and harness threw a glitter over the calm, youngish lady in the back.

" It's Miss Rudith, ma'am! " Seely said eagerly.

As the carriage passed, the two women glanced at each other through their veils. The lady on the purple cushions never changed, but Tacey, I thought, flinched and cheapened a little. Just for a moment. Then we were past and Tacey was herself again, but Castle Rock didn't interest her any more. We crossed the street and followed the carriage down. It stopped at the Watrous horse block. When we passed on the other side, Miss Rudith was talking to several ladies. She had slipped off her coat in the sun and I saw Tacey's eye expertly noting every detail of her dress.

I remember the next day, which was Sunday, Gaye gave Tacey a letter when he got up. It had come to him in care of the saloon. She glanced at the postmark and was instantly on her guard.

" How did anybody in Socorro know where I was? "

" I never even wrote a postal back," Gaye said. " They must have heard where I was working."

Tacey plucked a reddish shell hairpin from her head, slit the flap, and withdrew a single sheet of paper. It had blue lines and was written in pencil. Her eye ran down the page so rapidly that Seely looked at me in admiration as if to say: Why, she can read as fast as Miss Pritchard! When Tacey finished, all the hard distrust had left her face. She looked up and her eyes were a warm blue-green.

" Bee's coming through! She's going to be married."

Gaye's face changed little or none, but I had the

impression he was distinctly disturbed. I remembered Bee well — Wee Bee her name had been on the door. She was the only one of the lot Tacey would invite to her room, soft armed and breasted, the youngest and least painted, with the blackest of hair and ready to tremble if you turned on her.

" Married? " Gaye's voice had a funny sound. " Who to? "

" She's marrying a mine foreman in Tombstone." I'll never forget the different, sweet, almost mealy-mouthed way Tacey said " marrying."

" Well, that's up to them," Gaye said after a while, grimly.

" They'll make a go of it," Tacey told him. " She can have her wedding right here."

" You can't do that," Gaye said in a low voice.

" Why can't I? She's told nobody down there. They don't even know where she's going."

I saw Gaye glance at me, then at Seely. From that time on he spoke in riddles. Tacey knew what he meant but, whatever it was, she wouldn't flare up at him now. I had never heard them like this before, Gaye the one who got hard and mad, and Tacey staying sweet and trying to please. Once or twice I had the notion that, talking about Bee and her wedding, they were really talking about something else, something that included Tacey and what she hoped for, but which some code or pride kept her from saying. Gaye seemed to know very well what it was and kept capably out of reach.

In the end Tacey was herself again.

" I'll have the best in town to marry them! " she defied him. Gaye looked grim and watchful.

"If you mean Judge Congin, he wouldn't come up here."

"That two-bit gambler!" Tacey scorned.

Gaye flushed faintly, in surprise, I think, and alarm, too. He watched when dinner was over, as Tacey hurried Seely and me into our best clothes.

"It's time," she told us, "you started Sunday school."

"Don't they have enough school during the week?" Gaye asked.

Tacey paid him no attention. She got out her pocketbook.

"Remember, one nickel's yours. The other's for collection. No pennies."

"Where's this place that you got to pay them to go to?" Gaye asked.

"The church the best people go to," Tacey turned on him fiercely. "The Episcopal. Have you any objections?"

Gaye didn't change until quite suddenly a moment or two later.

"So that's what you're up to?" he said, almost under his breath. "You wouldn't dare!"

"Why wouldn't I?" Tacey flashed at him. "I've been wanting to send them for months. I may go myself as soon as my hair's out."

What she meant was the real color of her hair, which she was letting come back again. When she went downtown she kept it under hat and veil, but at home there it was for us to see. At first the new shade had showed itself only a short way above the roots. Then it spread in curious streaks. At last her head was like an Easter egg daubed with clashing hues. Seely and I liked the real shade so much better than the make-believe that we wondered why in the first place she had ever changed the soft chestnut red to a hard yellow stain.

It was my notion Seely wouldn't take to Sunday school, or Church School, as they called it. Indeed, Tacey herself must have wondered. She took us to the big dim door and almost pushed us in. But she needn't have pushed Seely. Seely gloried in the chance to wear her new dress and to sing in front of so many people. Her mind, that had known the newest string of cuss-words, now took to Church School hymns and she would startle me by singing one lustily around the house.

Gaye stopped talking against Church School the minute he saw how much Seely liked it. Always he stuck up for her now as his good-luck piece. He would even play the melodeon for her if she asked. "You sing the air, and I'll follow you," he'd say. Usually I went out when they started it. Having heard it once in Church School, to listen to it at home was too much. But if I had my chance now I would like to see and hear them again — Seely standing by the melodeon, her hard little voice singing: "Fight on the right side. Hell's damnation shun. Death to alcohol till vict'ry's won," and on the stool gravely accompanying her on the keys, fetching in all the faithful little chords, my brother, the faro banker at the Empire Saloon.

Tacey didn't tell us when she answered Bee's letter, but she took us along when she called on the vicar, as the Cousin Jacks called him. Tacey was nervous enough. She had dressed herself almost as severely as in the White Palace. Her voice and ways as we went down O.K. Trail were mannered and subdued. I'm sure she had to force herself up to the vicarage door. Never before had I seen fear in her eyes, or tremendous respect. Although Timmy was big enough to stand on his feet and even walk good distances, she lifted him up in her arms as we came on the steps.

" You knock, Nugget," she said.

The vicar himself came to the door. I had seen him in Church School, a tall gaunt man in a black robe, his high forehead like a meerschaum pipe smoked very dark by the Southwestern sun. But I had never been so close to him as now. He wore black trousers and vest and a turned-back white celluloid collar. No coat. His face had dark blue scars and veins where coal dust had filtered under the skin during his anthracite miner days. Bisbee liked him tremendously. The miners called him Brother John.

" Yes? " he rumbled, putting his great forehead down inquiringly and opening and intensifying those blast furnaces of eyes.

I was glad Tacey had Timmy in her arms so that she couldn't twist them.

" Would it be possible," she asked in the lowest voice I had ever heard out of her, " for you to marry a friend of mine? "

Brother John relaxed and laughed. Why, he said, he thought when he saw us standing there it was some accident. He remembered Seely and me, patted our heads, asked a few harmless questions, set down the date and hour in a notebook with red edges, and invited Tacey to service next Lord's day. He said he would be delighted to perform the ceremony, and all the way back through the gulch and up O.K. Street and Trail we moved in triumphant processional.

The last suit Tacey had made me wasn't good enough for the wedding. I had to have a new one, gray again, but a check this time, bright enough to be seen across the gulch, like the cap we once saw on Senator Watrous by his fountain. Tacey and Seely had to have more than that. For a week the snippings lay all over the front-room floor and I had to watch when I stepped from my bunk so that my bare foot wouldn't be in a pin or Tacey's tracing wheel or, worst of all, the pegs of her pleating board. This was summer vacation, with plenty of time to run in the gulch, but once the goods came, Seely forgot the gulch was there. All day and part of the night she stayed drunk on silk and velvet and patterns and long pieces of whalebone cut with the scissors to size and then soaked in boiling water for the needle. In their sister sessions she and Tacey were thick as two thieves, with Seely sitting close as she could get, learning to hem and gather and sew a straight seam. With their faces over needle and thread their talk ran by the hour, how so-and-so did her hair and so-and-so made her clothes, what this one had on underneath and what that one did to her skin. And when she wasn't at that, Seely sat on the floor, cutting doll clothes from the scraps with Tacey's buttonhole scissors and paper dolls from the French fashion plates for her play wedding. " You can have the old magazine," Tacey had told her. It

had been in the White Palace. Now Bee should see
only her new ones.

When the dresses were done I wondered where I
had seen them before. Tacey's was the palest silk
with slightly darker velvet bands, and Seely's an
exact miniature of the larger so that when they tried
them on together they looked like real mother and
daughter. That night in bed the dress on Miss
Rudith last month by her carriage block came back
to me. That had been brown and these were cream,
but the three had the same shape and fling, the same
sleeves and bows and paired bands at wrist, throat,
and hem.

Bee was due on the train that had fetched us to
Bisbee. Gaye said he would sleep downtown after
work that night, and Tacey left Seely with Timmy,
taking me with her to the depot. It was dark and the
train didn't come. I wanted to sit and doze in one
of the little fenced-off seats of the waiting-room, but
I had to walk up and down the platform with Tacey
till the train puffed in. It was very late and by the
dim yellow oil lamps Bee looked pale and frightened
as she came out on the open platform of the car,
peering this way and that into the strange ob-
scurity.

" Here we are, Bee! " Tacey called out cheerfully.

Bee's face lighted up.

" Deary! " she called back, hoarse with relief, and
when the brakeman handed her down, they flew to
each other.

She had only a suitcase, which I manfully lugged,
for I was nearly eleven now. It had almost nothing
in it. She had given all her White Palace things, she

said, to the girls. I thought Tacey stiffened faintly
at the words " the girls." Just seeing Bee made me
want to ask about Midnight Rose and Rowdy Kate,
but Tacey never mentioned them. By herself she
kept the talk going through the usual crowd of
miners, drunk and sober, at the mouth of Brewery
Gulch.

Bee said almost nothing till we reached the com-
parative quiet of O.K. Street. Then her voice
trembled.

" Are you cold? " Tacey wondered.

" No, just nervous," she said, very low. " You were
wonderful, Tacey. You know, I wouldn't have dared
this if it hadn't been for you."

" Don't you ever dare to think such things! "
Tacey flashed at her. " You'll make as good a wife as
any and better than most."

" I wish I could feel that," Bee whispered.

" And a mother, too! " Tacey asserted.

" Oh, I never would dare," Bee said, so low that
I could scarcely hear her.

" Bee Hosmer, you're a fool if you don't," Tacey
snapped.

When we climbed the steps, she pushed swiftly
ahead to light the lamp. Bee had stopped just on the
threshold and, as the light came on, I saw her look
slowly around — first at the familiar things like the
ostrich feathers and strip of velvet on the wall, the
colored afghan over my bunk, and the books and
little red lamp on the table — then at the new things,
the picture of Paris, the chair with the tufted otto-
man for the feet, and an ingrain carpet with roses
over the entire front-room floor.

" I can't believe it's all yours, Tacey," she said.

Tacey pushed into her own room, taking the suitcase. She came out with her hat already off and put away. They talked on their feet for a while.

" I want to show you something, Bee," she confided mysteriously. " We'll have to be quiet." She led the way to a door off the kitchen, stopping with one hand on the latch and lowering her voice. " I had this room built on last winter. They had to blast it out of the rock. Sh! " She pressed the latch with her thumb and held the lamp in the other hand so Bee could see.

Tacey had gone to the store so often the last week I thought it might be something I didn't know about, so I pushed my head in, too. All I could see were the matting on the floor, a bureau toilet-water bottle sewed up in an embroidered blue satin cover, and Seely and her baby brother asleep in bed. Timmy's little nose stuck straight up, and nothing was to be seen of Seely but the back of her head and her dark hair over the white bolster. For an extraordinarily long time Bee and Tacey stood there stretching their necks and whispering. When they closed the door Bee's eyes shone as if Tacey had showed her a vein of gold in the blasted rock.

Tacey sent me down with Bee in the morning to meet the Tombstone stage. Before its red wheels rolled down the canyon, I had showed her the smelter, the company store and the Empire Saloon. Bee stood strained and motionless as a man with big shoulders and a scar down his jaw slid over a wheel and came quietly toward her. His new blue serge suit was chalky with dust. Then I ran home.

" What's he like, Nugget? " Tacey put to me as I came in.

There was something about Tacey this morning that puzzled me. The two chickens roasting in the oven were enough to flush up her face, but it wasn't that. The imperious hardness had softened. She seemed anxious, hoping, eager to please. She asked me twice if I had seen Gaye. This was a new Tacey. Back at the White Palace she was the one that Bee had looked up to, but since breakfast this morning it seemed the other way round. When Bee and her man came, she got Bee out in the kitchen. " I think he's grand! " she whispered and hugged her, which was no more like Tacey than myself. She had manzanita branches hanging in the front room and flowers from Mrs. Calvera's garden in a jar on the table and out in a bucket in the shade behind the house a bouquet for Bee to wear. For the first time in my life I felt unhappy for Tacey and yet I didn't know why.

The wedding was for " high noon," Tacey had told us. About eleven thirty Gaye and Dappa Duke came. Even before he entered the house, his laugh floating up through the open door broke the stiffness. He was a fairly old man now, with an untrimmed white mustache and beard, but he was tall and imposing as a patriarch, his cheeks apple red, his sharp blue eyes twinkling. It was a name known from Butte to Cananea. When Dappa Duke had the faro concession, gamblers knew the bank would never go broke. He subscribed to no creed but his money had built one of the first Episcopal churches in the territory. I myself had seen the vicar stop and talk to him on Main Street in front of all.

Dappa Duke knew just the proper words to say about " the happy bride " and " lucky groom " and " making the twain one." When the vicar came, he found them all laughing togther.

" Welcome, Brother John and your little black book! " Dappa Duke boomed sonorously. " I'm here to see that you do a good job."

" Ah," the vicar said, delighted. " So you smelled the wedding banquet down in Brewery Gulch."

" Na, na," Dappa Duke laughed. " I came to kiss the bride before you."

" Well, I'm glad you're to hear some holy words," Brother John said. " You know, there's more joy at the coming of a sinner than all the souls who are saved."

The little front room now fairly vibrated with people and the event. But Tacey never forgot for an instant. At the proper time she drew the bride and groom to the kitchen door. As the whistles from the smelter and a half-dozen shafts ceased blowing, Gaye pressed the keys on the melodeon for a short march and Bee and her friend moved awkwardly the few steps across the room to where the vicar stood under the plume of ostrich feathers. Then Gaye got up from his stool and he and Tacey solemnly joined them.

I think that, whatever it was that Tacey thought or hoped for, she didn't give up until the moment the vicar began speaking. Then a change came. She seemed to listen, but when you looked close, her green eyes were faintly gray and far away. After that

she didn't glance at Gaye any more. But once while
the vicar droned, she turned her face peculiarly toward Bee beside her, and her eyes examined her in
quiet detail as if searching for some mark of distinc-
tion or good fortune she had not perceived there
before.

Tacey's dinner was fancy enough for the Watrous
mansion. Even the safely married bride and groom
were nervous at the style and very careful with the
china Tacey had bought only last week. Brother
John and Dappa Duke were the liveliest ones there.
Dappa Duke told a long story of the arrested smel-
terman who, when Judge Congin asked his occupa-
tion, said: " Y'm a Svede," Brother John matched
it with a story of the Irishman chased by a bear.
He was full of stories as of roast chicken. The only
other one of his I can remember was about the telegram that came to a man at the hotel. It was from
his wife in New York and read: " Jerry died last
night." He was such a nice man they hated to give
it to him. The proprietor himself took it sympa-
thetically in. To his surprise the man laughed. " You
can't guess who Jerry was? " the vicar said, his eyes
twinkling around the table. " It was his wife's dog."
Dappa Duke laughed heartily but Gaye stirred as if
restless with all this, and wanting to tell a real story.
Twice Tacey's eye had to halt him. I think she didn't
trust him. She was afraid he might tell a shady one.

I thought it a great success for our small house
and wondered that Tacey felt no prouder. She ruled
all with an efficient hand and forgot nothing. When
the vicar said he had parish work to do, it was Tacey
who took him to the steps and thanked him and

pressed something into his hand. We knew the bridegroom had tickets for the afternoon stage back to Tombstone, from where he and the bride would presently start for Alaska, and now the rest of us went down to see them off.

Before we left, Tacey slipped something into her handbag and down on Main Street she gave Seely and me handfuls of rice to throw at the pair as they climbed into the stage. I had noticed Gaye and Dappa Duke laughing together and now Dappa Duke pulled a folded cloth from his frock coat. He held it while Gaye tacked it to the door panel. There it stretched and hung where everybody could see it, a big white banner stitched in Tacey's heavy black thread:

HONEYMOON

People on Main Street began to crowd up on the boardwalk to read and smile. Passengers stuck heads from the windows to see. The driver grinned and climbed up on his high box and the red coach went up Main Street with the white banner still on and Tacey and Bee waving handkerchiefs at each other until round the turn.

" May a ripple never mar their happiness! " Dappa Duke boomed.

Gaye stayed downtown and Tacey led us home. She moved up O.K. Street with unconquered style, even when Timmy's fat legs grew tired and she had to carry him. But once up the steps she asked us to be quiet. Seely and I watched her go into her room. We were a little startled. We had never known Tacey to lie down in the daytime before.

Chapter 9

THE HALTED EARTH

IT wasn't blasting that shook the house that day, only the Cornishwoman climbing our steps. She labored around to the back door where Tacey was ironing.

" I seen ye go by last month with your fine gown and wedding party. Will they be happy, you think? "

" Why not? " Tacey came back at her, a faint warning in her eyes.

" Ain't your hair coom out grand and true, ma'am! First time I seen it changing I thought o' my first hoosband. The man was silver as the old lady on the dollar. I think he worried over all the men around me when he was underground. So he dyed it. Then we coom here. When he stopped dyeing it the whole gulch coom to me one by one. ' Your man's bad sick,' they told me. ' Never did we see a man get gray so fast.' "

Tacey's iron kept going. It was a big flatiron, heavy and unwieldy in my hand, but in hers light and expert as a black swan, wheeling here and wheeling there, never the same path twice, slipping over a sea of wrinkles and leaving a wake of satiny smoothness behind. The Cornishwoman watched her under her eyebrows.

" Can I speak to ye in private, ma'am? "

Tacey's eyes rose level.

" You can say it here, Mrs. O'Dell."

" With these young ears wide open as zebrays? All right if ye say so." Her eyes glinted. " Ye was in a sporting 'ouse once, wasn't ye ma'am? 'Old on, now! Ye told me I could say it. I just coom to tell ye the ladies on Quality Hill got up a committee. They're going over ye with a fine-tooth comb. If ye peep out the front door ye can see the marshal cooming this way now."

I heard Gaye, who had been stretched on my front-room bunk, get up and go to the front porch. When he did not return, I judged he was watching someone below. Tacey's iron was at a seam and her face careful over it, but you could see that she had steeled.

" Be careful of the loose step as you go down, Mrs. O'Dell," she said.

" Oh, I'm going," the Cornishwoman said and still she wouldn't go. One lid dropped shrewdly. " Ye want me to take the young ones till it's over? "

" No." Tacey had stopped ironing. It was so ominous and still that the hair at the back of my neck twitched but the big Cousin-Jack woman leaned forward unaware.

" Do ye deny it, ma'am? "

Tacey could have turned up her flatiron or left it on its holder, but she carried it in her hand as she stepped around her ironing board and I swear I saw a pair of orange flames back in her eyes.

" Are you accusing me, Mrs. O'Dell? " she asked.

" Never a word! " the Cornishwoman ejaculated and we could hear her scratching against the side of the house as she went.

" This is what you get from Bee! " Gaye told her.

" You better go downtown and keep out of this," was all Tacey said.

It gave me no shame at the time to see my brother get his coat and hat and jog down the steps, leaving Tacey to face it alone. Indeed, I thought it was wisest this way. Tacey could handle it better herself. I remembered the woman they had tried to put out of a house on Chihuahua Hill last year. The land-lord and two men had gone in to pull her out and she had chased them down the steps with a butcher knife. Day and night they had laid in shifts to lock her out, but the neighbors fetched her water from the hydrant and flour from the store. In the end the landlord had to give her up, and that, I knew, was what would happen to anybody who tried to fight Tacey.

Seely came running back from the door.

" Andy Coe's on our steps, ma'am! " she called.

Tacey ordered her and me to sit quietly in the kitchen. When a knock sounded, she went to the door herself, with Seely and me behind her.

The Bisbee marshal stood there. He had once been a big man but was now only frame and skin, with a throat of tanned gristle and a blue flannel shirt to keep him warm even in summer. He looked so ancient and slow it was hard to believe that this was the man who had beaten the draw of outlaws from El Paso to Tombstone. His was a famous name, but all that was over now and his assignments today were a broken head in a saloon or stabbing in some lumber yard. The paper still called him Marshal Coe, but everybody knew, and he knew, that a town constable, subject to the whim of small politicians, was all he was.

Now he took a folded paper from his peaked hat. Tacey's green eyes flashed down its opened length and then at him.

" Am I a thief that you serve me something like this? "

" No, ma'am," he said humbly. " The ladies just want to talk to you. They're coming to the judge's office."

" Why don't they come to see me? "

" I don't know, ma'am."

" Well, you can take this back to Judge Congin," she said and handed it to him.

He just stood there looking away from her with dulled eyes as if he had no use for this business either but had been enduring ignominy himself for the last year.

" If you'll let an old man talk to you, ma'am, you'll only make it worse for yourself. This is a summons, and if you pay no attention, the judge'll order us and the sheriff's office to come and get you the best we can. I've seen a good many go like that and it went bad with them before and after they got there. If it was me, I'd sooner go down quiet and take what they had to ask me with my head up. I've seen plenty come out of it all right."

I watched Tacey's face. There was no fear in it. Indeed, as she glanced back into her front room with her pictures on the wall, fashion magazines on the table, and Timmy playing with spools on the floor, it seemed to give her something. She had been here several years. She had done no wrong. She glanced down at Seely and me and I saw her grow calmer. She was respectable and secure. She wasn't afraid. If it had to be, she would go down and show these women what kind of person she was.

" I'd never move a step with you or the sheriff," she told the marshal quietly. " But I'll come by myself today when I can."

" I'll trust you, ma'am. It's at two o'clock," the old outlaw-fighter said humbly and left.

Back in the house Tacey told us to scrub and dress in our best, so we knew we were going along. Our hands moved so fast and hers so carefully today that we were ready before she had Timmy and herself washed, combed, and dressed. I had always thought her strict enough with us before, but that was nothing to the way she went over us today, making me wash the curlicues of my ears again and doing Seely's hair over with her own brush. Then with Seely and me a little ahead and Timmy in her arms for the steps, we started from our front porch.

We passed the little white house on O.K. Trail with the stained-glass squares around the front window. From inside, Seely had told me, the gulch looked red, blue, or yellow depending where you put

your eye. We passed Mrs. Walker's boarding house
with the bureau out on the second-story porch summer and winter. A miner stood out there in his un-
derwear shaving now. The hill began to pitch very
steep, and the muscles of your legs ached from holding back till you got down. We passed Union Hall,
always plastered with bills. Pretty soon we were in
Brewery Gulch with the Watrous carriage standing
on the corner and the Mexican coachman staring
past all the miners loafing around it.

Seely knew the way. She took us quickly and
proudly into a dirty hall. Straight back was the
weekly *Miners' Journal*, with a hand press clanking.
Seely's feet led swiftly upstairs to the police office,
and the marshal took us through the hall to Judge
Congin's office.

Entering that long dim room with its yellow
woodwork and old red wallpaper and smelling of
spittoons and musty staleness, it was almost like
going into church or Sunday school, the same feel of
homage and reverence in the air and of ladies seated
and whispering. And the man behind his desk ruled
over all like the preacher in his pulpit, except that
the judge seemed the more righteous and holy. Only
a justice of the peace or police judge he was, but he
always slightly frightened me and I saw Seely watching him, too, a tall, inordinately thin man with
ragged gray goatee and mustache. He dressed like a
lawyer in very light clothes which did not entirely
hide his almost fleshless knees and shoulders. He
looked emaciated with some slow disease, but not
even that, whatever it was, could extinguish the soft
deliberate power living behind those yellow-stained

eyes and mustache. Gaye said he stayed up half the night at the Empire gambling with two-bit chips.

" Come in and close the door, Andy," he ordered.

Tacey had swept in quietly. There were more ladies there, I think, than she expected. I saw her glance down over us with satisfaction that neither one had got a dirt spot on. I walked beside her with a great deal of pride and remember my surprise that none of the ladies said to another: " Don't they look nice! "

" Up here! " Judge Congin drawled to Tacey and just the way he nodded her to the chair when she approached, without looking at her, fetched faint red to her cheek. She had stiffened slightly.

" Sit down. You are — ah — " his hand hunted slowly over the green baize that covered his desk like a billiard table. Then he held up a small piece of paper in his long fingers — " ah — Tacey Crom-well? "

Tacey inclined her head.

" What's your real name? "

" Tacey Cromwell," Tacey said in a low, proud voice.

" You're not married, then? "

" No, sir."

" Am I to understand you're not the legal wife of Gaye Oldaker? "

" No, sir," Tacey said firmly while the rows of dresses on the chairs rustled with delicacy, I think, and disapproval. The judge, as if he had unearthed something of merit, made two or three underhand brushes at his mustache.

" These children." He lifted his eyes at her.
" They make their home with you? "

" They do." Tacey had eased slightly and sat more erect.

" Have you a legal order from Tombstone to adopt them? "

" No, sir."

" Why didn't you go to court? "

" I thought what they needed was food and clothing and school and Sunday school."

A murmur rose from the ladies, but, to my anger, it was not in sympathy or approval.

" You weren't afraid to go to court? " the judge asked.

" No, sir."

" You aren't afraid of this court? "

" No, sir."

The judge's pointed, yellow eyeballs seemed to pierce her.

" Let me ask you something. What was your real purpose in taking in these children? What use are they to you? "

I saw Tacey pale slightly.

" What use are anybody's children? " she said in a low voice. " I wanted to give them a home."

" You thought you could give these children a home? " he asked incredulously.

" Not only thought but gave! " Tacey corrected him. " For two years, and more."

The judge showed his stained teeth through his ragged mustache. In that moment I hated him.

" I'm speaking of a Christian home," he said. " A woman with your history — "

"Judge Congin, may I interrupt?" a voice asked.

"Certainly, Miss Rudith." His manner instantly changed.

The ladies turned their heads like seals to listen to Senator Watrous's daughter. Without, she was gentle and plump so that you felt her flesh would give most places you pressed your finger. But inside you could tell she was firm as a church.

"I think, Judge Congin," she said, "these two older children should not be present."

It was the bitterest disappointment to Seely and me when the judge had us sent out. Seely refused to budge till Tacey ordered her. Then she obeyed, but I saw her glare at the ladies as she went. Behind us Tacey did not try to stop us. What her feelings were I don't know but I felt her watching us till the door shut us off. Once outside, I saw through the narrowing crack that with Seely and me taken away she had changed. That stiffness of Socorro and early Bisbee days was coming over her again. Then the door closed.

Out in the police office there was a cabinet with many things for us to see — a rope that had hanged a man in Tombstone, a Filipino knife black with dried blood, little sacks of marihuana that looked like hay, the hair halter of Geronimo from Fort Bowie, and much more. People went up and down from the street all the time. Upstairs the prisoners stamped and sang. From the stairs came the strong zoolike smell of the jail. And at the front hall window we could look down into Brewery Gulch and see William Williams's dog Curly sitting out in front of the Reception Bar sprawled down in back and sunken on his front feet, the dejected picture of an old dog that had spent most of his life waiting in front of saloons. When Chris Gulam's shepherd ran eagerly in and out under the swinging doors looking for Chris, the old dog gave him a dull dispassionate look. The shepherd was young. There was much that time would teach him.

An hour of this and we had had enough of the police office. By supper time we were sick for the sight of Tacey. Andy Coe had long since been sent out and for the last hour some of the leading citizens of Bisbee had been going into Judge Congin's office. Seely and I tried to get a peep whenever one went in, but Tom Noonan, the constable's helper, kept yanking us back. There were loud voices from time to time now, but Tom wouldn't let us listen. His face was scarred by a fall of rock. Black and wiry, still quick at forty, you could tell he hated our guts because he had to tend two kids.

When at last the marshal let us in, the sight of Tacey shocked us. It didn't even look like her. When we had left she was the Tacey we knew, with her hat up and veil flying. Now something terrible had happened, something that we couldn't even guess. Her hat and veil were off and her streaked red and orange hair uncovered for all to see. At home her head was always like that, but every hair combed trim and neat and snapping with electricity. Now the life had gone out of it. Her forehead where it met the hair was not the young Tacey we knew. She looked beaten, not with sticks but by words and thoughts. You could tell she had fought but these women had fetched in their men to see the deed through.

Only Tacey's eyes were alive, and they fairly devoured Seely and me as we came in. When Seely saw her, she ran.

" What's the matter, ma'am? " she cried.

" Seely," Tacey said in a low unfamiliar voice, " I want you to do as I say."

" I want to go home," Seely complained loudly.

" Listen," Tacey said. " One of these ladies wants to take you and brother — "

" Not to stay! " Seely interjected quickly.

" You'll do as I say! " Tacey begged, very low.

The cruel lumpy look I knew so well began to choke up Seely's face.

" I got to go home with you first, ma'am," she said. " For my things."

" I'll send you your things," Tacey told her with difficulty. " Will that be all right? "

Seely gulped and nodded, but she didn't move from facing Tacey. You could tell she couldn't understand why Tacey was doing this and yet she had guessed that Tacey was saying good-by. Neither spoke. They didn't kiss or shake hands. They just stayed that way looking at each other and I could read Seely's eyes as plain as anything. She was begging Tacey not to carry out this terrible and inexplicable blow, asking her what she had done, pleading with her not to send her away. Always Tacey had taken care of her before, even when the whole world had fallen with her father in the back stope. Tacey had done everything then. Tacey could always manage things. What terrible thing had happened to change it now?

But Tacey only sat there beaten, silenced, her eyes holding Seely as if it was herself as a child she had there in front of her and wouldn't let go and that, it came to me in a flash, was a secret of the bond between them.

The women coughed and Mrs. Ness, whose husband ran the Ness Hardware and Mining Machinery Company, moved out from among them with Timmy in her arms. She was an iron woman with bust, waist, and hips corseted in and out like an hourglass.

" I'm sure you'll want to stay with us, Celia," she said, her strong face below her pince-nez broken into a smile. " God gave us no child of our own."

Seely looked with bitter eyes at Tacey.

" I won't go with her," she warned.

" Obey your new mother, child! " Judge Congin ordered.

" That old battleaxe's not my mother! " Seely cried.

" Well, indeed! " Mrs. Ness gave a flustered, indignant glance around. " It's time they had a different home."

Behind Seely's back the judge was making mysterious and encouraging signs to two of the ladies, who took firm hold of Seely's hands.

" Now we'll all go and see your fine new home! " they said enthusiastically.

" Let me alone! " Seely panted, bracing her feet. And when they tried to drag her toward the door, she fought back. " Let go of me! " she bawled. " Let

me go, you dirty bitches, or I'll bite off your lousy
fingers! " She thrashed around now like an alley cat,
kicking, snapping and gouging till in self-defense
they had loosed her.

"Oh! " Mrs. Ness was saying. She had drawn
back, her fingers over her ears.

" The child will learn different language in your
house, Mrs. Ness," Judge Congin promised.

"Not in my house," Mrs. Ness moaned. " I've
changed my mind."

" You must remember — " the judge began.

" I do not want her! " Mrs. Ness declared, every
word a stab. I had never seen such radiance on
Seely's face. She gave me a triumphant look although her eyes avoided Tacey's.

" The child can't go back to Brewery Gulch! "
Miss Rudith said, distressed but emphatic. " There
must be someone to take her." She stood there, trim
on her feet, in a tailored silk of fashionable black
and white stripes. Earnestly she glanced from face
to face, while one after another they excused themselves for lack of room.

" I'll take the boy for a while, like I said." Pretty
little Mrs. Herford glanced nervously at her husband. " But I have no room for the girl."

Still flushed and panting, Seely ranged herself beside Tacey. I thought I had never seen her prettier.
I had been this close to her a thousand times and
had never noticed before that her eyes weren't really
dark. They were gray. It was the shadow of her inky
eyebrows that gave them their smoky black look.

I saw Miss Rudith's eyes on her, too.

" Fortunately, Father and I have the room," she

said gravely. " If none of you can manage, I shall take her myself."

The ladies murmured shocked protest, but none offered to relieve her. Seely's glow was gone. She turned with desperate face to Tacey, in whose eyes a fleeting hope had died.

Tacey met the occasion with an effort.

" You've got to go, Seely," she said, pitilessly.

Miss Rudith stood there plump and kindly, yet royal and not to be denied.

" Shall we go now, Celia? " she asked.

When after a minute or two Seely had stumbled blindly out, Tacey found her own hat and veil. Her eyes were as if she had never known me.

" Don't try to come along, Nugget," she warned.

She rose, very thin and strained, almost slatternly, looking around, I think, for Timmy, but the baby had been carried away. Although I didn't know it then, we would never see him again. In a moment she was walking stiff and ungraceful toward the door. I tried to go after her, but the hard arm of Mrs. Herford's husband, the superintendent at the Higgins shaft, stopped me.

When they took me down, Tacey was a distant figure moving up the street alone. I could hardly bear turning away from Brewery Gulch. As I walked toward Quality Hill, between Mr. and Mrs. Herford, such a longing and homesickness came over me that I felt I couldn't stand it to live any more.

In front of the Watrous mansion Seely was just getting out of the carriage. Miss Rudith had driven old Mrs. North home first. I saw Seely stare at the great strange house behind its iron fence. Then she gave me a look, and I understood as if she had spoken. We jerked loose and our feet hardly touched the rock as we raced down the middle of the canyon toward Brewery Gulch.

If we had had any sense, we wouldn't have gone that way but cut up behind the pay office and out to Zacatecas Canyon to hide. Instead we ran straight for the police office and Tom Noonan heard them yelling. He almost got us, too. With him and others at our heels we fled up Brewery Gulch into that honeycomb of alleyways, of private and public steps, and of trails crossing and crisscrossing. I let Seely take the lead and she ran up the Michovich stone steps, off on the Lewises' wooden steps, and over the pole handrail to Mrs. Freyno's cribbed yard. From here we crawled by the long side of Mrs. Otis's house, whose windows you couldn't look in or out of for all the flower cans, with their paper long since off.

It was a marvel to watch Seely. She knew by instinct just where to work up along the shelter of the Rinnans' slant-slatted fence. We sneaked through Mrs. Calvera's sunken garden with orange and lemon trees in tubs and up the long steps of Mr. Gratz, the old German with the white patch across his big nose. We didn't know where Tom Noonan was now. We could hear only the peaceful sound of the old German playing his piano to make his canaries sing. We could see the five or six cages through the window along with bags of potatoes, a shelf of red books, dirty garden tools in the corner, the yellow piano, and no carpet on the floor, all in the same room.

O.K. Street was clear when we came to it. We could have run straight home, but that would have been the way of a fool. Over the street in one jump we went, and half-way up the long steep Kresak steps we stopped to watch the Kresak dog coming down. That was a sight to see, the brown short-haired dog almost standing on his head, his eye always on the step below, like an acrobat walking downstairs on his hands, tending strictly to business and never minding us. Where the Kresak steps stopped, the Jones steps went on to the little house that was yellow as far as the top of the windows where the paint had given out. From there on, weathered gray had to do.

This was the highest house on Chihuahua Hill and we threw ourselves on the ground a little to ease our chests and legs. Nobody was at home but the pigeons in their boxes on the shed and we watched them teeter out on their shingles and take off. From up here they needed only to spread their feathers and drop into the gulf and after a while to sail back with hardly a flap out of their wings.

" If I was a pigeon," Seely panted and stopped.

She had seen a small dot that was Tacey coming up O.K. Trail. She must have gone the long and loneliest way around. She moved slowly, turned, climbed the long steps to the empty green house, and the door closed behind her. I looked at Seely, then we hurried across the ridge above us. When we crawled back over Youngblood Hill the house lay straight below us. We could have spit down the chimney. We kept out of sight behind acorn trees, yucca and manzanita bushes. Some places were so steep we had to go down backward. The last twenty feet we climbed from hold to hold like goats down the blasted rock face of the hill.

I thought Tacey surely would hear us, but we heard her talking and found that Gaye had come back and must have waited for her in the house. Through the window she still looked as she had when she left the police office, her back thin and almost slatternly. One shoulder seemed lower than the other. Every now and then she went into the bedroom and when she came out, left clothing and small things over the front-room bunk.

" But they got to give reasons! " Gaye told her.

" I'm not a fit woman to have children around," she said bitterly and went back after another load.

" I teach children to curse," she said when she came out. " I'm foul and filthy. Soon I'd have Seely working in some crib up the line." Suddenly she turned out through the kitchen for Seely's room and we had to dodge under the sill till she went back.

" I told you Socorro was too close to Bisbee," Gaye reminded her.

" That had nothing to do with you," she said. " And I wasn't good enough for you either."

I know now that she meant marriage, and Gaye, of course, knew it at the time, for he moved uneasily. Tacey's thin back slanted there by my bunk as she sorted the things into piles. One pile was in the armchair, and that was Seely's. One moved to and fro on the rocking-chair, and those things were Timmy's. One stayed in a corner of the bunk, and that was mine. The fourth lay on the melodeon and, to my surprise, I saw that this was Gaye's.

"What's the idea bringing out my things?" he demanded.

"I contaminate children," Tacey told him. "I don't want to contaminate you."

He stared at her, angry, baffled, and a little frightened, I think.

"How could you get along? I'll stay with you," he said.

She just looked at him, a pitiful and pitying look, and he knew, and Seely and I knew, he wasn't going to. She was laying his things in his suitcases first. The way those hands worked sent a chill down my back. When she buckled the suitcase straps, she tied up my bundle in a newspaper, and after mine, Timmy's. Most of these things she had made for us herself, sewn them with her own hands. Last came Seely's bundle. Tacey's fingers seemed unable to knot the cord. Twice it broke.

"You can take them now," she said, and her voice was quiet and cruel. "They'll know where to take Timmy's. They're hiding out by the back door."

Seely and I gazed at each other.

"Look here!" Gaye began.

She looked at him, and God grant I never see a face like that again on someone I love. It was dead, like the face in a coffin you can talk to all you like but it will do nothing you say.

"Don't bring them through here," she said. "I'm going to my room."

At the strange sound of the bar of her latch turned back against the doorjamb, Seely rose and stumbled in.

"Ma'am!" she begged, shaking the latch and pounding the door with her small fists.

"Take them away!" Tacey's voice inside rose to a scream.

Seely turned to Gaye with an agonized look. Slowly she picked up our bundles and Gaye his suit-cases. The hills of Brewery Gulch, when we got to the porch, were dotted with watching neighbors. Below us the marshal and Mr. Herford were coming up our steps.

Chapter 10

QUALITY HILL

For days Tacey's scream stayed in the back of my mind. I'd find myself sitting up in my bed at night with the sound in my ears, and it would take me a few moments there in the dark to remember where I was. Then I'd feel sure that something had happened to her up there in the gulch. I was sure I had heard her, not in a dream, but real in my ears.

Lying down again I'd think of Mrs. Shepko, who had lived near the cribs. When her man ran off with another woman, she went to cook for Old Forty-One till he'd come back. She was a big Slovak or Pole and they called her Little Joe. When he didn't come back by Christmas, she went up on the roof with a bottle of poison in her hand. Then she called everybody out to give them good-by. Seely and I saw the crowd and got there in time. All the hookers were in the street from Number Nine and the Majestic and the Mint and Canadian and the cribs up the line. They argued with her. They promised he'd be back by New Year. They offered her more wages. They held up pieces of their best clothes she could have if she'd come down. But they couldn't stop her. When some tried to sneak up to her the back way, she drained the bottle.

For ten days now I hadn't seen Seely except at school and Sunday school. The woman who took Timmy, I heard, had moved to Utah. And the closest I got to Brewery Gulch was the post office. Mr. Herford gave me strict orders to run straight home after school, and his wife kept me playing around there till dark, when I had to come in. Mr. Herford was a powerful, medium-sized man with a silent jaw and truculent eye. One look from that and you said yes, sir, and no, sir, and put aside any monkey business. Mrs. Herford was soft as he was hard. It seemed perfectly natural that they had no children. They were two entirely different species. At the supper table, ashamed of the silence in front of me, she would try to get him to talk, but all he had to say were brief statements of fact about the mine. Once two new Finns were beaten up by his Irish day-shift. That's all the story he could make of it and then it was days afterward when the Finns hadn't shown up for their pay. Another time they had been hoisting water all day and the rope and guide had got wet and broke, dropping the bucket six hundred feet and killing two miners, but all Mr. Herford would say was: " Bad, yes, but could have been worse. The same thing happened up in Ophir once and killed six men."

Those days I didn't know if Tacey was alive or dead. Brewery Gulch got to be a kind of dream in the back of my mind. I could walk down Main Street and not believe there was a place like that just over the hill. If Mrs. Herford made any afternoon calls, she made them while I was at school. She was always there when I got home, and at night when she went out, Mr. Herford sat smoking his pipe over company papers at his home desk. The Herfords lived on Quality Hill. They had a white house with a porch all around. It wasn t wide, but just to have that much porch you couldn't use made me homesick. I felt alien with the fancy butter knife at the table, the sofa's burnt-leather pillows, the crayon portrait on a bamboo easel bigger than I was, and the silver dish full of cards in the hall. The furniture of my room was a girl's pale, flaxen shade. Sooner than have Matt MacCachy or any other Brewery Gulch boys see my shame, I would have cut off a hand.

But I had one stroke of good fortune, when the Bisbee Social Club and the Episcopal Ladies' Guild met on the same evening.

" You won't be afraid to stay here alone for a while tonight? " Mrs. Herford asked me. " I'll leave the hall lamp burning."

" You wouldn't stay all night? " I said quickly so she wouldn't think me too eager.

" Well, it might be — eleven o'clock. Perhaps Mr. Herford will come home earlier."

" I wouldn't mind that long," I said, keeping my face dead as Gaye's behind his faro bank. Everybody knew that the Episcopal Guild seldom broke up until after midnight and the Bisbee Social Club kept people awake till daylight.

Mrs. Herford sent me to bed early and left. I could still hear Mr. Herford dressing in their bedroom. Then he went downstairs and I smelled his pipe for a while. When the front door closed, I sat up, and when the gate clicked, I jumped out of bed.

Up to this time I had seen four states and territories, but never had I found a place sweeter to me than Brewery Gulch that evening. Once you turned through the narrow entrance, it seemed a thousand miles from Quality Hill, like another land and clime. The air tonight up into the deep gulf was clear like wine and through it broke all the small twinkling lights of houses on the hills and the sounds of life and living. Listening with an expert ear, I could name every gang of kids playing from Youngblood Hill to Opera Drive and back over School Hill.

" Yanh, a-yanh; yanh, a-yanh; yanh, a-yanh-anh! " a boy gave the Chihuahua Hill yell.

" You're dead! " bawled a kid. " I shot you deader'n hell."

" Whee-ee-ee! " A child stamped up and down a porch screeching like a neighing horse.

" You bugger, you! " a girl screamed.

" Say-dee! " called Mrs. Neuffer.

" Twenty-three, twenty-four, twenty-five, all around my base knocked off! " Sadie Neuffer droned.

Up along the line phonographs were whining and player pianos galloping and here on Brewery Gulch Street a fight was starting. It was good to hear hobnail brogans on boardwalks again and smell the strong ferment from the double row of saloons. It

turned out to be just a Cornishman thrown out of
the Butte Bar, where only Swedes and Finns dared
to enter, but it put everybody in a friendly humor.
I spoke to all I knew, even to Dummy Glim, whose
big flat shoes came flop, flop, flop down the middle
of the street with his baggy pants swinging front and
back.

The men always answered him short and looked
the other way, but the women would be sorry and
talk to him.

"Weah Feely?" he said, stopping and beaming
at me in the light from Tooney's Bar.

"She don't live with me any more," I told him.
"She lives down in the Watrous mansion."

"Sua," he nodded, shrewd and pleased. "She wig
wady now."

"I don't know," I said.

"Wim know." He pointed to himself. His hands
felt through his clothes till he found what they
hunted for. It was an old belt buckle with the tongue
gone and worn shiny from his pocket. He passed a
dirty lump of a hand over it tenderly. "You wiv
Feely. Say Wim wive."

"I'll give it to her," I told him.

The small eyes in that pudgy face beamed at me
again; then he went down the street, flop, flop, flop.
When I turned toward O.K. Street, I threw the
buckle away. Then I saw Gaye.

I hardly knew him at first. The lighting was dim
here. He was ahead of me and carrying something,
his hat pulled down far over his eyes as if he didn't
want people to know him. Just the way he walked,
I thought it must be he, and when he passed the

lone lamp-post on O.K. Street, I could see he was carrying his two suitcases. He had on his best suit of heavy brown stripes that always reminded me of Rope Twist, a favorite brand of miners' chewing tobacco. I let my feet drag and stayed behind him. He heard me but waited till we came to the Pythian Castle to look around, so that the light from the restaurant window would fall across my face.

" Where are you going? " he wanted to know.

" Where are you? " I asked him, keeping my distance.

He just looked at me for a minute and went on till he reached the foot of Tacey's steps. Here he let down his suitcases and waited for me.

" What do you want up here? " This time I could tell he meant business.

" What do you? " I came back.

" Does old Herford know you're out? "

" Go and ask him if you want to know."

" You better go back! " he blazed at me.

" You can't make me! " I dared him.

He made as if to rush me and I ran. When he climbed the steps, I climbed a safe distance after. As he neared the top I noticed that his feet slowed and I thought he intended to come for me, but when he reached the porch he stood there a moment as if reluctant. Then he knocked. After a time a light warmed the tiny front room, the bolt sprang, the door opened, and a person stood there holding the familiar little red lamp.

It took me a second or so to realize it was Tacey, and then I reproached myself that I hadn't come before. She was in her nightdress and blue kimono embroidered with white daisies. That blue kimono I knew as well as the bunch of ostrich feathers over my bunk, but not the person in it. She had grown thinner. I do not mean fragile or delicate. Rather her flesh was white putty.

" What do you want? " she said, and her eyes and voice were cold at us as strangers.

" Tacey! " I cried and ran up to her, but she backed away from me, and Gaye came in, too, hastily fetching the suitcases, setting them behind the rocker, and then closing the door.

" They gave me off tonight," he explained, not looking at her. " Everybody's at the Social Club. Don't you feel good? "

" Why not? " Her glance warned him. " I'm fine. I was just sewing in bed for a change." I could see the thimble on her finger and the litter of patterns, pins, scraps of cloth, thread, and ravelings over the front room. She looked at me. " Do the Herfords know where you are? "

" They were gone when I went, Tacey," I said meekly. " So I couldn't say anything."

She understood me perfectly and if she had done something about it I would have felt better. But it wasn't worth the trouble tonight.

" How are you getting along? " Gaye stammered, meaning how was she making a living.

" You needn't look after me," she said, a dead woman outside and in her eyes. " I got along before I knew you. I guess I can afterward. You're the one to think about. You didn't do so good beforehand. I wouldn't bet on you now."

I turned to Gaye. In his new tan, button shoes, his

best mottled vest, and with a toothpick slanted up prosperously out of his mouth he looked good to me. Only his red tie hung amiss. Tacey's quick fingers had always knotted it for him as he liked it with a bow on top and flowing loose below. I wondered who had tied it for him now.

"The trouble with you," she went on, and her voice was level as for an enemy long unforgiven, "you got cheap aims. If it wasn't for me, you'd still be hammering the piano at the White Palace or some worse place. You need a woman to get you up. And you'll find plenty to take you. But don't make a fool out of yourself again like you did with me. I'm a bad woman. I'm no good." The white flesh around her mouth was extremely bitter. "I curse and teach kids to curse and go bad. But you're a man. You're not hurt. Not one of those women had a bad word against you. They only felt sorry for you." Her heavy eye glazed on him. "Do you think if I'd be you and you me, I'd have anything to do with you?"

"What do you mean?" Gaye asked, staring at her.

"I've had time now to think this over," she said. "You can take those suitcases back down, because I'd never take you back here." Her eyes were cruel, final, the left a little distorted as if it didn't look quite at him. "If you weren't such a fool, you'd pick out somebody more than you. Much more. But I know what you'll do, so I'll pick one for you. She'll marry you when you're up and right where you should be. I mean Rudith Watrous. She's the one I'd go after."

"You're looney!" Gaye brought out, but he

looked frightened. Indeed, just the flat, matter-of-fact way she had said this astounding thing had sent shivers down my back. Tacey went on:

" She feels sorry for you, I could tell by what she said." Tacey's lip twisted. " She pities you the way I roped you in and kept you down. She can get you the job you ought to have — in a real bank. Nobody can fool you with counterfeit or count money faster. She isn't as far above you as you think. Her father was a common miner once. When you were up the other day, you told me what she said when you fetched the kids back. What was it? "

" Nothing," Gaye muttered.

" Didn't she hope you'd lead a better life from now on? Didn't she say you could come and see Seely? You used to be fond of Seely. Why don't you call and see her? " It was the first time Seely's name had been mentioned this evening and just the way Tacey's inflamed eye looked at Gaye you could tell she would have sold her soul for the same chance.

" I'd never go there! " Gaye snarled, but his lips were white. I had never seen him so shaken.

" Why don't you raise a mustache and hide that ugly mouth! " Tacey told him coldly. " Take out that toothpick. Get rid of that ugly suit. Get a good one at the tailor's over the bank. You'd look a lot better in a derby." She had started to walk around him now like she used to inspect Seely and me during a fitting, but just the way she did it and what she told him chilled me inside. I had thought that if I ever saw a spark or curl of fire in her again, it would fetch the heart bounding up in me. But the fire I saw far back in her eyes tonight was the fire from the pits of hell.

Gaye just stood there, angry and yet petrified, I think, by the emerging evidence of Tacey's pitiless plan. I remembered again what the girls at the White Palace had told me — how he never showed any feeling — that even the tears of the weepers rolled from him as off a duck's back. I thought they should see him now. He stood there outraged and stunned. His eyes said she was crazy and he wouldn't stand for any more. And yet he and I both knew Tacey was one to reckon with. He had done so long what she had told him, he would have a hard time to do otherwise now. Even those times he had stood up for his rights and talked back to her were just make-believe for his manhood's sake. In the end he had always given in.

From my bed that night in the silent Herford house I could see two tall chimneys on the roof-top next door. They were like a man and a woman facing each other bitterly against the dark sky. They seemed to be with me all night in my sleep and I was relieved in the daylight to see that the resemblance had vanished.

I had forgotten all about it when Mrs. Herford broke me the news that Gaye was coming. He was taking me to see Seely. He had talked to Mr. Herford. I'm sure Mrs. Herford didn't altogether approve of his coming around and yet she liked me to be calling at the Watrouses'. I remember I sat on the porch in the sun, tight as a board in my Church School suit and new, coarse-ribbed black stockings when a strange man came, ill at ease, through the

gate. Then I saw it was Gaye. The brown suit and
hat were gone and with them the scarlet tie. He
looked uncomfortable in a hard black derby, a new
gentleman's walking suit of some dark weave, with
a vest of the same color and a blue tie that seemed
to choke him. I found out afterward he had bought
it at the company store already tied with a curved
wire fixed underneath to hook over his gold-headed
collar button.

He asked merely if I was ready. I had never seen
him stiffer. He acted as if he knew this wasn't going
to work and he was making a fool of himself only
to prove it to Tacey. Going down the canyon together, I don't think we exchanged a word and both
of us stopped, glad enough to watch Professor Tyn-
dall, the mind-reader, give a street demonstration.
He drove, blindfolded, a two-horse buggy down the
canyon, holding the reins in one hand and his other
on the wrist of Mr. Cryle of the Bisbee Improvement
Company, who was the only man who knew where
a small American flag had been hidden. The blindfolded professor turned out for wagons and people
as well as if he could see. At the post office he suddenly brought the buggy to the boardwalk, felt his
way down and into the library side, still blindfolded,
and presently came to the window tearing off his
bandage and waving in triumph the red, white, and
blue.

Once it was over, Gaye stiffened again. He gave a
long, doomed look around the hills till his eyes fastened on the mansion behind its iron bars. Then we
moved up to the door with arched glass above it,
set in fine carved wood.

" Is Miss Seely home? " he asked doggedly of the Mexican maid.

Peeiing past her, the great hall bewildered me, broad, with carpets and settees and rubber plants set in tubs, and noble steps with a polished railing rising to unguessed-at regions. Gaye must be desperate coming to such a place, I thought, and would be still more so till he got out. The maid closed the door, or nearly, to go back somewhere. I saw it open a little for an eye to peak out. Then it widened and Seely stood there, in polka-dot dress with shiny black belt and tied cuff-strings I had never seen before, finely woven black stockings, and shiny slippers, and holding her head stiff on account of all the careful curls hanging down.

" Gaye! " she suddenly cried. You could have almost heard her at the fire house. " I didn't know you with that mustache! Where's Tacey? Why didn't you bring her along? "

" She's sewing," Gaye said, very low, his ears the color of carrots.

" Aren't you coming in? " She dragged him over the marble steps. " Oh, I like you with your mustache! You look so good in it."

" He's raising it to get a job in the Bisbee bank! " I told her.

Back in the hall I saw Miss Rudith herself step out with a book in her hand to see whom Seely was making such a fuss over. I can remember just the trim, easy way she stood in that elaborate place, so anybody could tell she was mistress and belonged, her plump finger in her book so she wouldn't lose her page.

" Oh! " she greeted us with a cool, formal little nod of recognition, the coolness, I think, for Gaye's profession, and the recognition for Seely's sake. " Celia, dear, don't you want to entertain your company in the sitting-room? "

I would have called it the lying-down room. It had three couches, no less, together with a piano, chairs, and a red carpet, and as I entered, the whole effect, if somewhat more worn and comfortable, was dazzling, scarlet, and grand as the Masons' Lodge Rooms which Matt MacCachy and I had once peeked into on the third floor of the Michovich Building. Gaye looked around rigidly and took the couch with a raised end to rest one of his arms on. I sat on the flat couch and Seely chose the scarlet one, from which she tried to make us feel at home, but we all seemed far away from each other as if perched on the seats of three separate ore wagons in the smelter yard.

It wasn't Seely I watched, however, but Gaye in this rich place. Glum as he was, the mustache Tacey had had him grow softened him here, gave his face an almost generous air. He seemed a different person. I know he wasn't listening to Seely's bragging, and yet that black, hair-covered lip made him seem gentlemanly and attentive as she told all about the Watrous carriage, the dresses Mrs. Rolls, the dressmaker, was sewing for her, and the great safe they had in the kitchen to keep all the wonderful food in.

" I could show you something upstairs you never saw before! " she bragged to me. " It's got a green tub so big even Miss Rudith can lie down in it. You can get hot or cold water, whichever you want." She hurried off her couch to bend over and whisper at me. " You don't even have to go outside when you have to. You can go right there. Don't you want to come up and see it? "

" No," I said shortly.

" Why don't you want to? I'll let you try it. I'll wait in the hall. If you don't know how to work it, I'll come in and show you."

I looked away, annoyed. Miss Rudith's shoes had long since vanished soundlessly on the thick carpets, but I could feel her in another room reading. From where I sat I could see across the hall through double doors into the parlor, vast, profound, and hushed as an empty church, with marble and gold lamps and the chairs and sofas shrouded in gray covers. And beyond that I had a glimpse of the dining-room with the huge bulk of a sideboard, half of burnished copper, and palms in the bay window.

Seely complained to Gaye: " He'll never do anything," adding an uncomplimentary name just with her lips. Then aloud: " You're not scared to play for me? "

" I can't here," Gaye said quickly.

" I'll sing for you! " Seely coaxed, her eyes hardening.

" She wouldn't like it," he refused, very low.

Seely put on a mysterious face and went out, not running as she used to on Youngblood Hill, but holding herself straight and moving along with her curls stretching elastically up and down. She came back the same way.

" She said you could! "

Gaye was sweating now. He gave me a hard look that we should never have come. Seely had to drag him to the piano. I had always thought he looked manly at the melodeon, but here against this great, square, rosewood thing he seemed crude, impotent, and uncertain. For a long time he kept twirling the massive red stool as if to put off the ordeal, and when he did sit down, he didn't look right with his hat off and I felt sure he couldn't play that way. But at the sound of the first cautious chords ringing through the room, he rode the stool a little easier, leaned back in his man's way, laid his head bit to one side, and his fingers ran swiftly through a trick he had learned at the White Palace, a showy gamut of chords on every scale from bass to treble.

Then he struck a familiar and homely Church School air.

" That's a good one! " Seely, standing beside him, said quickly, all her words strung together to start singing it in time, but he was beginning to feel his oats now and staved her off with a fancy little interlude. As he came around cleverly to the starting chord, she smiled at him in friendly conspiracy. Then her hard little voice went up like a small, bare, freckled fist through the room and house.

After the second chorus I heard a delicate round of handclapping and looked up to see Miss Rudith standing in the doorway.

" You never told me you could sing, Celia! "

" Doesn't she sing here? " Gaye asked and wished he hadn't. He got up quickly.

" I never knew it! " Miss Rudith declared.

Gaye stood uncomfortably. He would rather, I

know, have left thinking Seely was happy here.

" Well, I've got to go."

" Don't go yet! " Seely cried, running to him and holding his arm with both of hers. " You just came."

" Mr. Oldaker will call again, Celia," Miss Rudith said, taking one of the child's arms in hers and drawing her gently away. She gazed at him with a new expression and, having noticed it so often in the eyes of Mrs. Herford, I could see now the promised birth of a moral which those days must never be left unsaid. " Did I hear that you are bettering your work? "

" He's getting a job in the Bisbee bank! " Seely boasted.

" Just trying for one," Gaye said humbly.

" You're not living in Brewery Gulch any more? " — this very grave.

" No, ma'am." Gaye lowered his eyes.

Miss Rudith stood here in the great sitting-room, solid, thoughtful, and gently triumphant, but the person I saw after a moment was someone who wasn't there at all, a slighter figure with putty-white face standing fiercely in a tiny room on Youngblood Hill, in her nightdress and blue kimono with white daisies embroidered on it, who didn't know her triumph at all.

Chapter 11

SONG OF THE ROCK

THE SECOND year I was at the Herfords', Gaye went up in the world.

The first year he lived at the Philadelphia Hotel and once a month doggedly took me calling at the Watrouses'. Sometimes he would play and Seely would sing and more than once Miss Rudith came in to talk a little and serve tea, in cups small and light as eggshells. You could see every finger through them and each was a different color inside. At the end of that year the bank offered Gaye a job, and he took it, Dappa Dick and Fred Downey, proprietor of the Empire, going on his bond.

Often when I went by on the boardwalk after that I could catch a glimpse of Gaye's mustache drooping behind the teller's window. Mrs. Herford thought it a great honor for my brother to be working in a bank, but the miners asked him what he had done to get put behind the bars. Of course, it was partly in fun, but partly in earnest, too. You could tell by their looks, they had trusted him at the Empire, but they would have to keep an eye open for him now. His faro bank had never failed to pay off every dollar it owed, which was more than could be said for all the financial banks that had gone broke through the territory, working hardships on thousands of widows and poor people.

My own private feeling, and Matt's, too, was that Gaye had gone down in the world. He complained bitterly once that he was no more than a clerk and had had more respect at his faro table. Then one night in March he walked into the Sports Club Saloon while Will Hendricks was losing heavily at the craps table. A big crowd stood watching and Gaye watched, too, for a while.

" Give me a turn! " he called out, elbowing in ahead of Hendricks and picking up the dice. But when he threw them, they went off the table in a spittoon.

Hendricks, owner of the great Border Cattle Company, cursed him, but Gaye coolly fished out the dice and called for a towel. Just the easy way he stood there silenced the crowd. It watched him quietly clean up the dice, turning them over under his practiced eyes. Before they were dry, their owner had left for parts unknown and the proprietor and floorman were at Gaye's feet. The story went over town how Gaye Oldaker had smoked out the loaded dice. He kept them at the bank and men came in just to see them and compliment him. It seemed that a bank teller was good for something after all, and at the next smoker they initiated him into the Bisbee Social Club.

It was a great honor and I wondered what Tacey thought when she heard the news. I had no chance to visit Youngblood Hill now and when I saw her on one of her rare visits downtown, she passed me as if she had never known me, except for a certain warning shape of her lips that if I spoke to her, I'd be sorry. I remember her very well one noon. Just a little earlier I had seen Gaye moving up Main Street with men calling to him from doorways and others walking along a way to hear his latest story and parting with a joke and a laugh. A few minutes later Tacey passed the same way, going to the Fair. She was alone. No one spoke to her and she spoke to no one. I wanted to cross the street and walk along with her on the boardwalk, but I didn't dare. Often after that I wondered if, had she to do it again, she would have sent Gaye away. She hadn't foreseen, I felt sure, how it would work out. She had stayed in Brewery Gulch sewing for the madams and high-class hookers up the line, while Gaye had gone his own way on Main Street. Every month the gulf had grown between them. One Sunday afternoon on the way to Church School I saw Gaye driving with Fred Lawrence and his rubber-tired open buggy to the Gun Club. Another afternoon, a hot one in May, he went to the Watrous mansion like a gentleman in a blue serge coat and ice-cream pants. But the final badge of his success was when the *Review* named him one of the officials for the Fourth of July Drilling Match. I knew then that the gulf between them had grown too wide for Tacey ever to bridge.

Each was in his proper place now, Quality Hill felt, and Miss Rudith was given the credit. Indeed, everyone thought Tacey finished, and the Herfords gave me freedom to visit Brewery Gulch again. Matt had entered the boys' drilling contest and Mr. Herford, who had once been a double-jacker himself, said I could join Matt in a double-handed team. Matt's father would train us. He had come home from Alaska the fall before. Matt hadn't seen him for three or four years. All this time the family had starved and gone ragged. Then one Saturday morning Matt's father had shown up, taken his wife and kids to the company store, and picked them new outfits from head to toe. Price was no object, and from what Matt told me, it must have been an orgy of buying, with the clerks running here and there and Matt's father standing like king of the prospectors, throwing gold eagles on the counter and ordering this and that with a beck of his thick finger. Matt said he had sold his claim in the Klondike for five thousand dollars. Most of the money was gone when he reached Bisbee, and the rest soon after. Soon he had to go to work underground at the Czar shaft.

It was strange to be back in Brewery Gulch again and not go up to Tacey's. Matt's father's place stood on a shelf of solid rock and we practiced drilling right in the yard. For one minute Matt swung the hammer and I held the drill, and for the next minute we changed around. After school stopped, we drilled mornings, and afternoons we sharpened our steel in

an old prospector's forge that belonged to Matt's
father. He was a thick, heavily moving man with the
powerful jowls and bloodshot eyes of a bloodhound.
The men said he kept few company rules underground, jumping the shaft when it suited him and
stepping on the moving bucket. But he knew single-
and double-handed drilling and he showed us how
to temper our steel, how to keep the drill from sticking, how to change over without missing a stroke.

"Hard and steady!" he'd keep growling. "That's
what eats the rock."

"Let them rest — they're tired!" Mrs. MacCachy
would say, coming to the back door.

"Rest!" he'd explode with ponderous indigna-
tion. "You've got to train like Bob Fitzsimmons."
Then back to us. "Go on, lads. It's muscle does it."

But when his friends came around, he'd forget us
for his favorite subject, the Klondike. Matt and I
would throw ourselves on the ground like dogs to
listen. Under the surface up there, he said, the icy
ground never melted, not even in the summer time,
and they had to build a fire every morning at the
bottom of their prospect hole to thaw it out before
they could dig. Matt and I would look at each other
and turn over on our backs. I still remember the
sensation of lying there in the searing June heat and
hearing of the everlasting ice in the Klondike.

I got to like the burly old man. More than once
when the fire in the forge wouldn't burn fast enough
to suit him, he'd break a stick of dynamite into the
flame as if it were no more than sawdust and never
a word to me to move although I were standing
right by. Sometimes he'd take a pinch of the powder

himself and Matt and I would gravely follow suit.
It tasted sweet like sugar. " Give you a bit of a head-
ache at first," he'd say. " But it's good for you. Like
the smelter. Those half-assed women on Quality
Hill want to kick it out of town. Why, that smoke's
good for the germs!" Once when the hammer
smashed part of my finger, he planked on a chew of
tobacco still warm from his mouth, then melted
tape and wound it hot around my finger.

But he was a hard trainer and the minute he left
for the three o'clock shift, Matt and I quit for the
day to attend to our hunger and thirst. Sometimes
the women at the cribs gave us two bits for running
some errand to the drug store, but usually we hunted
whisky bottles. The Butte and Shattuck bars paid
a nickel a pint and three half-pints for a dime. If we
were lucky, we battened on bananas and Sweet Cap-
orals and the soft drinks Mrs. Hopple made to order
at her little store by stirring colored powder in glasses
of water. If it was still early, we rode burros out
Mine Road. At the Lowell shaft tank we'd take off
our shoes and walk barefoot up the cool pipe and
swim in the yellow copper water that gave you pim-
ples if you stayed in too long.

It seemed some days very much like old times, but
it really wasn't. Brewery Gulch wasn't the same. I
couldn't get Tacey out of my mind. Whenever I'd
start feeling good, I'd look up and see her little
house on Youngblood Hill without a sign of life
around. She was there I knew, seldom going out,
Tacey who liked movement and excitement more
than any of us, while I was training for the Fourth
of July, and Gaye and Seely were always on the go,

and moving up in the world. More than once I went
around by O.K. Trail just to get the feel of passing
her steps again, but I never had the courage to go
up. I felt sure she wouldn't want me, that just to see
me in her little front room would make her sensitive and unhappy and bring the hard hurt out in her
face. She certainly knew that Gaye by this time was
calling alone at the Watrouses' and that people were
coupling his name and Miss Rudith's, just as she
had said that night. But it must be a bitter draught
to her now.

Then Matt told me something I couldn't believe.
It was Sunday and we lay behind our stable on
Quality Hill.

" He's still going up to her," Matt said.

" Who is? " I demanded.

" Your half-brother, to Tacey Cromwell."

" You're loony! "

" He's been all along. I seen him with my own
eyes. He goes in the dark of the moon and keeps
his hat pulled down over his eyes. But he can't fool
me."

What Matt said profoundly disturbed me, although I couldn't have told you why. When we
lived up there, everything seemed proper and all
right. But now I felt incredulous and uneasy.

" You think I'm lying," Matt said. " Next time I
see him, I'll come and get you."

But when he came, I never tumbled to what he
was after. It was two nights before the Fourth. I
was tired from our last day's drilling and ready for
bed. A knock sounded and Mrs. Herford opened
the back door to find Matt standing there.

"Can he come out with me a little, ma'am? " he begged.

"Tonight! " Mrs. Herford said. "Why, it's almost nine o'clock."

"I know, but we got a champion up the Gulch, ma'am. He can tell us how to win. Tomorrow he won't be there. I'll have him back in ten minutes."

"Well, he better be back before Mr. Herford comes," she said.

I got my hat and we ran down the canyon.

"Who is this champion? " I panted.

"It's your half-brother," Matt said. "He's up with her again tonight."

I didn't entirely believe it and yet I felt a wave of shame for Gaye sneaking up to her like a dog in the night. I didn't know now if I wanted to go up or not. On O.K. Trail we went quiet except for our breathing. There was no moon. The light from windows told us where we were, but I could have found my way blindfolded. My feet knew every twist and turn. Tacey's steps hadn't changed. They gave where they used to give and rocked where they used to rock and squeaked where they had squeaked before. But I had never had this feeling on the steps before tonight.

I had an idea where we'd find them, and, although he said nothing, Matt must have thought so, too. I think it surprised us both to hear voices coming from the lighted front room and to find the window and door open. As we crept closer we could see them both standing there.

"Stop rattling your money that way! " Tacey was saying, and her caustic voice was a tonic to me.

" Everybody knows you're a banker now. And don't lean back on your heels down there. It's cheap."

Gaye said something I couldn't hear. Tacey's voice came sharp.

" You can be proud you're in it. You're an official. Nugget's the one I worry about. You think he'll ever go to college now after you've left him drill? "

Gaye spoke very low.

" Don't say tony! " Tacey flashed. " Say nice or stylish or genteel. All you have to do is stand up on the platform and keep time. You're always telling stories. You ought to be able to say a few things to the crowd. You'll get used to it once you're up."

Gaye started to speak again.

" That's what you told me about going to see Seely! " Tacey interrupted. " What would it bring you? "

A little silence, then in another voice:

" Is Seely going? " she asked. Gaye had his back toward her, but I could see her face and her look of secret yearning as she spoke Seely's name bared her soul and made me ashamed to be out on her porch spying on her.

I turned and started fast down the steps and Matt followed. Down in the Gulch we just said so long and went our separate ways. But I knew that if Seely came to the contest, nothing could keep Tacey away.

Even before daylight you could have told it was the Fourth by the peculiar machine-quiet in the town. The smelter and shafts had laid off after the three o'clock shift last night. Of course there were other signs, too. All night they had been shooting in

Brewery Gulch and on Bucky O'Neil Hill. By daylight the sound rose like a battle all over town, with
the pip of cap pistols, the burst of torpedoes, the
popping of firecrackers singly, in strings, and under
cans. You could tell the fast staccato of five-shooters
and six-shooters and the heavier blasts of shotguns.
But the backbone of the din was the giant powder
sticks of the miners. They roared in every gulch and
on every hill, constantly shaking the town.

I could hardly eat my breakfast. Under all the
hell let loose you could hear a low rising hum that
worked on me like pins and needles. When I hurried
downtown, the canyon was alive with people and
Main Street stood walled with decorations. People
had stayed up half the night. Not a house without
flags crossed or hanging from porch and windows,
with bunting wound around the posts. The Fair had
a cloud of tiny flags over it, and at most other stores
great colored streamers flowed down to the wooden
awnings. The second and third floors of Liberty
Hall were a sweep of color, but the saloons drew
the eye. The front of the Empire was a five-pointed
red, white, and blue star. Others had circles and
horseshoes, and the Sports Club had a spreadeagle
with the whole staff of mixologists, gamblers, floor-
men, and proprietor out in front for their picture
in the morning sun. Going down Main Street a
thousand flags hung together in the still air, and
when a breeze came, the whole canyon fluttered.

All early morning people kept pouring into Main
Street from the side gulches. Trains, stages, and
teams fetched them from a score of near-by camps;
and two automobiles had come all the way from

Tucson, making the hundred miles in two days. In the crowd you could pick out Mexicans, Swedes, Russians, pink-cheeked lads from the tin mines of Cornwall, Italians, Slavs, Serbs, and natives of every kingdom in Europe. Confederate veterans wore their colors, and peddlers selling souvenir badges and striped canes moved through the jam.

I looked for Tacey during the early foot-races in front of the grandstand. Matt and I were up a new spiked telephone pole and could see everything, but if Tacey was there she was hiding somewhere in the crowd. Every window and balcony on Main Street was crowded for the parade. At the head marched the Grand Army of the Republic with a fife-and-drum corps, and then for half an hour or maybe an hour came squads of soldiers from Fort Huachuca, Rough Riders and Arizona Rangers on horseback, ball players from Cananea in their uniform, and the fire company with its new hand-drawn chemical engine. The Redmen marched in feathers, the Eagles with their band blaring, and horny hands held aloft banners of the Western Federation of Miners and the Ancient Order of United Workmen. Four automobiles were in line, including the two from Tucson, and a score of horse-drawn floats bobbed and wobbled from the battleship *Oregon* to the Bisbee Improvement Company's " Tell the Telephone."

It was late before the drilling contest started. The engine with the car of rock had gone off the track behind the company store, but hundreds of brawny miners put their shoulders to the flat car and ran it out in the plaza. I had seen it down near the depot the last days, as had nearly everyone else. It was a cube of Gunnison granite with scaffolding built around it, and the sign said it weighed seventeen tons.

The crowd was the biggest I had ever seen, even in my dreams. The *Review* counted it at ten thousand souls. They choked the plaza, hung on all the near-by roofs, and the hills around were black with the overflow. Fine-dressed women watched beside grimy miners. Over all in the still hot air, such breath of beer and whisky hung, you could close your eyes and swear you stood in the Empire or the Sports Club Saloon. And those were the days when a saloon had the reek of a distillery, far from the pale lavender scent of a drinking-place today.

The miners cheered when the first team climbed up to the scaffold. The three officials were already there — Gaye to keep time and figures, Tom Deeny of the B. and K. to check the time and take the measure, and Lew Cadwallader of the G. and L. to say whether it was fair or no. Tom Deeny held the megaphone and chopped the air with his other hand for quiet.

" Drilling contest for the championship of the world! " he bawled. " Seven-eighths steel. No swedge steel allowed. Hammers not over eight pounds for double-handed and four for single-handed. Time of contests fifteen minutes. Any hammer in the air when time's called can come down. First double-handed team, Ross and McGuire from Butte, Montana."

For what happened from then on for a couple of hours you will have to ask some of the old-timers and not me. I was nearly paralyzed that this was for the championship of the world and Matt and I were in it. All that followed had to pass through a thick fog in my brain. The longer our turn to drill held off, the better for me, and the roars when each team or man finished made me sweat for being that much nearer. Not till night did I understand that Campbell and Gardner of Lowell had broken the world's record with forty-one and twenty-six thirty-seconds inches, although my own ears had heard Gaye call it through Tom Deeny's megaphone.

Later years they had the boys first and the double-jackers last but now it was the other way around, and when the single-jackers finished, prizes and bets were paid and the crowd started to rush for the saloons.

" We still got the boys' match! " Lew Cadwallader bawled through the red funnel, but the crowd went anyhow, or most of it. The sun was hot that day, only a few miles from the Mexican border, and they couldn't wait for the cold beer.

" Don't ye want to see the young ones drill? " Matt's father, angry, boomed after them, but I didn't mind. The more that went, the more of my nerve I would get back. Besides, Miss Rudith and Seely were in sight now. Their house stood only a stone's throw around the bend, but they came as befitted the Watrouses, in the shade of their carriage.

The two other teams drilled first. Both stood bigger than I but not than Matt, and the pair from Chihuahua Hill did the better with twelve and twenty-one thirty-seconds inches. Then came Matt's and my turn and we climbed the scaffolding with

Matt's father scrambling after, taking care not to spill his can of water, for he was our chuck tender. Some of the men by now had had their fill of the saloons and came streaming back to see what the kids could do.

I was stripping off my shirt when I saw Tacey. It struck me in the face and the heart, too, when I saw that she had come not straight across from Brewery Gulch but around by the railroad. She looked very stylish in a tan linen suit, but unsure of herself and nervous. For a moment she stopped behind the shelter of a clump of people, but when several turned their heads, she came on out into the merciless sunlight. The car and granite block hid the carriage from her for a moment, and when she came far enough to see it, she stopped dead at the sight of Seely in white organdie with a black velvet belt and a great white hat sitting beside Miss Rudith on the purple cushions. Seely waved to me and I waved back. I waved to Tacey, too, but her eyes were fixed on Seely.

" Come on, lad! " Matt's father growled at me.

I saw Gaye glance impassively from my light arms and shoulders to Matt's more impressive ones. He was built after his father. His hair was sandy and some ancestor far back must have been a sturgeon, for golden blotches stuck to his skin all over him like scales. Now he made his speech the way the grown men had.

"We're out to break the world's record!" he called out, sounding shrill, and a half-hearted cheer came from the crowd.

I was unwrapping the drills from the packing and

laying them handy on the rock. Taking a short starter steel I pecked at a likely place in the granite and waited. Matt tightened his belt, spat on his hands, and gripped his hammer.

Gaye raised his hand with no more notice of me than if I was a stranger from the Klondike. For a moment my eyes sought Tacey, and it gave me something to see that she had her handkerchief up with white encouragement for us both.

" Time! " Gaye called.

Before Gaye's hand dropped, Matt was down with the hammer and then it was click, click, with granite chips and dust flying and between every blow my fingers turning the drill. Matt's father had spread himself flat on the rock with his can and now he began to let in a little water from the hose. Chuig, chuig, chuig, the drill began to talk, with water flying in my face. Matt was by far the stronger, but I the quicker. Like lightning I had been churning the drill. Now at his father's coaching I threw it out and slapped in a longer steel before the hammer came, raised myself on one foot, holding the drill with one hand and getting a grip on my hammer with the other. Then at a word from Matt's father, down Matt came, spent, and up I shot, fresh, and my hammer hit the steel without missing a blow.

A nice little cheer came from the crowd at the change, but it died soon, for the sound of my hammer on the drill was not the same as Matt's.

" Bear down, lad! " Matt's father was growling, spitting out the mud. " Slower and harder. Sixty a minute. Remember the winners drilled the slowest. All right, Matt, get ready to change."

Most of the fright I had had for the people was gone now. There was no crowd any more, no Bisbee, nothing but Matt and me, this rock of Colorado granite, the six legs and shoes of the judges, and Matt's father flat on his belly, his face streaked and one eye closed with granite mud and wet from hair to shoes with the splash from the hole that came now in a steady spray. This was the world and the only world that was, and when we threw out a worn drill we let it go and hit where it pleased, usually into the crowd.

" Churn her! " Matt's father was saying. " Watch his hand. All you got, lad! Muscle does it! "

His was the one voice in my world. Matt and I had only grunts. A grunt to swing and a grunt to churn and a grunt to change up or down. And now my world began going around and around like the geography always said it did, but I never believed it before. My chest tore as if that was what Matt had been hitting with the hammer. I felt glad that boys were not men with fifteen minutes to go but only ten. I kept no count and toward the end I thought every change must be the last. Then when Gaye called: " Time! " I was too far gone to know human speech. I got up reeling and they had to fight with me to take my hammer away.

I saw Tom Deeny kneeling down to stick his measuring rod into the hole, and Matt's father close by watching. It looked like a tamping stick. The stick came out, he looked at it close and put it down again. Then he lifted it and spoke to Gaye, who brought up the red megaphone.

" Double-handed team of MacCachy and Old-

aker! " Gaye called out, calm as checking a column
of cold figures in the bank. "Thirteen and one
thirty-second inches."

It had no meaning for me and I wondered why
Matt's father threw away his can and the crowd let
go with a good cheer. In the carriage Seely was
bouncing up and down. My eyes went to Tacey. She
was waving her handkerchief. Her face looked like
old times and that told me everything was all right.
It is strange what a good feeling will do to the face
and body. That thin, slattern stiffness had gone. She
didn't know now quite what she was doing, for she
came flushed toward the carriage crying enthusiastically to me, but I couldn't catch what she said.
Seely called something, too. I saw Tacey smile with
blinding radiance at Seely, and Seely smile with
excitement at Tacey. Right then something inside
of me melted and for a minute I thought we were
still all happy together back on Youngblood Hill.

" Fifty cartwheels! " Matt said, giving me a clip
that nearly knocked me off the rock.

To hell with that, I thought, my eyes still on
Tacey. She was almost at the carriage now. In half
a minute they'd be together. I waited to watch
Tacey's face when she talked to Seely. Then Miss
Rudith saw her coming. She pulled Seely back to the
seat and spoke to Manuel. The coachman pulled
up the lines and the horses swung. Tacey had
stopped and it's good she had, for the carriage almost struck her as it wheeled around. For just a
moment she and Seely looked in each other's eyes as
the wheels went by.

With my shirt in my hands I saw that look I knew

so well go from Tacey's face. No sound out of her
or the crowd either, just the hoofs and wheels putting her in her place. I tried to pull on my shirt, but
I couldn't find the neck hole and my right arm
wanted to go in the left sleeve. When I had it right
and the tails tucked in, Tacey was half-way across
the plaza toward Brewery Gulch, moving thin and
alone through the men, the one arm swinging rigidly and too far as if, in some way I did not understand, it was her weapon against the world.

Chapter 12

THE MOSS–ROSE DRESS

FROM what Matt told me, Gaye was seen up Young-blood Hill until the week before the engagement dinner. After that no one in Brewery Gulch saw him on O.K. Street again.

A six o'clock dinner meant something very special those days, and this one wasn't held at the Watrouses', but in the newly finished Copper Queen Hotel. It didn't only announce the coming wedding but that Gaye was now assistant cashier at the bank. However, what impressed me was all they had to eat. I still have the clipping from the paper Mrs. Herford cut out and gave me to keep. At the end is the menu the paper got from the chef. It reads a little odd in places today: Consommé entassé; relishes, olives, chowchow, salted almonds; entrées, salmi of duck au chausseur and prime ribs of beef with Yorkshire pudding, garden peas, potatoes au gratin; cold asparagus tips à la mayonnaise; bisque ice cream and strawberry shortcake; Bent's crackers, soda crackers, fruit, raisins, nuts; St. Julien punch.

When Mrs. Herford read it aloud at the supper table, Mr. Herford kept right on eating his hash and fried potatoes and merely said: " Is that all they had to drink? "

He and I saw eye to eye on the wedding, I am sure, although we never exchanged a word about it. When the day finally came, we both had to walk to church, with Mrs. Herford drawn up like a turkey hen between us. You could tell how much more impressed she was than merely going to church to worship God on Sunday. I had to wear a suit fresh from the shelves of the company store, stockings still sewn together when I put them on, a shirt never pulled apart from starch before, and a stiff straw. Going up the hill in front of everybody I felt like a board planed and painted with gilt and ready to be nailed to the back of a pew.

The wheels of the carriages were already stopping at the church door and men and women in their best stepping down, while groups of miner women and kids stood watching from School Hill. In a double-breasted white vest Fred Lawrence met us at the door and ushered us up to a front pew where space had been saved. I knew few of the backs or sides of the heads around us. They belonged to important people from Eastern cities, from Arizona mining towns and Phoenix and Tucson. Even Mrs. Herford seemed nervous up here. I could see Seely across the aisle with Miss Rudith's aunts and cousins

from Cleveland. The whole thing was meat and
wine to her. She fluttered her handkerchief at me
when I came and then paid me no more attention.
All through the church fans were moving, ladies'
hats nodding, feather boas twisting. The sibilants
of silk and lips rose and the reek of perfume floated
around me so that I could scarcely breathe.

Even Gaye, when he marched down the aisle,
seemed like no brother of mine in a frock coat without a wrinkle and dark gray trousers with silver
stripes. Tom Head of the big Cananea ranch moved
in step with him, and when they got to the altar
railing, they nudged each other nervously to the
right position, like vestrymen who had never been
in church before, taking up the collection.

But Miss Rudith when she came on the Senator's
arm had no such uncertainty. This was her and her
father's church and all these prominent people her
relatives and friends. Things might seem strange
to me, but not to her. This pomp and pageantry,
the candles burning and the organ playing, Gaye
and Mr. Head like fashion plates, the bridesmaids
butterflies, and herself in ivory sheen, lace, folds,
and tucks brought for her by her cousin from Paris,
its long train held up by two small nieces behind,
the bridal bouquet in her arm and the wreath of
orange blossoms on her head — all these were right
and proper and in their perfect place. I didn't look
at the scene more than I had to. Most of the time
I let my eyes come down no lower than Brother
John's bald head. I counted the colored squares in
the window above the altar, the feathers in the an-

gel's wings, and the bumps on the stone that had been rolled away.

When Brother John closed his book, his scarred face was beaming. While the organ pealed and everyone surged toward the bride and bridegroom and Mrs. Herford chattered excitedly to neighbors how beautiful it was, I wormed for the door like a night creeper coming up for air and dew. Outside, the fresh air, sky, and hills were unbelievably like heaven. Below, I knew, waited the Watrous mansion with a room choked with wedding presents. There were the tea sets and toilet sets, candlesticks and cut-glass dishes, laces and table linen, silver pitchers, card-receivers and table service and things without end. Just the thought of them sent me toward Brewery Gulch where every rusty can and broken bottle and unpainted miner's cabin looked good to me, even Davy Calahan half drunk already at noon. I laughed at miners coming heavy-footed down the middle of the street, taking copies of the weekly *Argus* from Crip Gorman, telling him to charge it and no pity for a man who owned two houses if he had only one leg.

The MacCachys' dinner was over, but Matt's mother asked if I didn't want something, and I sat there at the kitchen oilcloth with Matt looking at me with the respect due a member of the Watrous family. Nobody seemed surprised that I'd sooner eat left-overs here than the wedding dinner. Nobody as much as mentioned the wedding. The nearest they came to it was after Matt's father went to his shift. Then Mrs. MacCachy said:

" Don't you want to go up and see her while you're here? "

" Who? " I stammered, knowing well enough whom she meant.

" While you got your good clothes on. Maybe she'd like to see you."

" She wouldn't," I said.

" It might cheer her up," Mrs. MacCachy said.

" Isn't she good? " I asked.

" You go on up," Mrs. MacCachy nodded. " Take some of these doughnuts along. But don't tell her I told you to."

With Mrs. MacCachy's little basket, and a clean piece of an old tablecloth over it, I went up Young-blood Hill. It was a hot June day. As I started climbing Tacey's steps I thought I heard a door close. When I came to the front door, it was shut, and not a sound when I knocked.

" Tacey! " I called, and went around to the back door, but that was locked, too, although the white slop jar stood cleaned and airing in the sun.

From both sides and around the gulch I saw women stealthily watching, and when I got down to the trail Mrs. O'Dell was waiting as if by accident.

" Oh, it's you. And she wouldn't let you in? " Her small eyes bored down at me to see how much I knew.

" She wasn't home," I said.

" Ho, she wasn't home, aye? "

" She'd let me in if she was home," I flared.

" No, not you or anybody else. Not even 'er best customers up the line. Won't sew a stitch for them. Stopped them all, she did."

A faint chill touched me that hot day.

" What's the matter with her? "

" It don't 'ave to 'ave a name to kill ye," the Cornishwoman leered down at me. " Ye expect her to go through the pits o' hell and not get singed? She's 'uman like the rest of us."

" Kill her, you said," I stammered. " Won't she get better? "

" Ye mean better or better off? " Her great face was like a triumphant piece of cast iron. " Aye, she'll get better one o' these days — when six men carry her down. And better off."

But with all her scaring me, the Cornishwoman was wrong. The next Sunday morning when Gaye and Miss Rudith were already on the Pacific Ocean, I felt a strange, indefinable air in church. We were standing up singing: " For we are His people and the sheep of His pasture," when I saw Mrs. Ness across the aisle give Mrs. Herford a look over her service book, one of those long, steady, almost paralyzed starings of the eyeball that, especially when seen through lenses, mean something grave, unlooked for, and to be warned against. Mrs. Herford sang on: " For we are His people," then turned to see for herself, and I noticed the word " hand " died on her lips. So I twisted my neck, too.

The night of the drilling contest when I had looked at the paper, I remember how my name in fine type had stuck out of the whole front page as if held under a reading glass. And today in the fairly filled church, the way one person held her head caught in my retina, guided the focusing muscles to it, and there was Tacey in a dark silk dress in the next to the back pew. She sat along the aisle. She had no book and the woman next to her had edged far away as she could so as not to have to share hers. Tacey stood rigid and her face was ghastly and thin, but her dress had fine pleats and slender ruffled stylish sleeves, and her black straw bonnet turned up with a daring tilt that I had seen only on Miss Rudith's cousin from Cleveland, who had brought the wedding dress from Paris. I stared for just a moment but her picture stayed on my mind as if on a photographic plate. I don't think she saw me. Her eyes were fixed with an expression I can't name on one of the front pews where Seely stood sharing a book of service with Senator Watrous. Seely was all of fourteen now, in a dress of soft dotted mulle tied behind and softer brown hair down loose over her shoulders from under the tailored straw she had worn to the wedding. When I listened, I could hear her voice in the singing congregation, and I think Tacey could, too. Once when we went down on the stools, I turned my head. Tacey was on her knees with the rest, and the anguish on that white face even a boy could not look at, but had to turn quickly as if his eyes had been on forbidden ground.

When I looked for her after the service, she was gone. She must have slipped away before the recessional so as not to embarrass Brother John, who always waited in the vestibule for the candles to be put out so he could shake hands with everyone leaving. Next Sunday she was in the same pew, and this time people must have talked and expected her, because she sat in the pew alone. I thought surely that would keep her away, but the following Sunday morning she was there again, and the next. Each time it seemed she had on a different dress and hat, but perhaps she had just changed the trimmings of the old.

In July a telegram arrived for me, the first I ever had.

GOOD TO BE BACK ON HOME SOIL AGAIN TAKING TRAIN FOR BISBEE SOON SO ANX-IOUS TO SEE YOU ALL LOVE

It was signed: " Brother and Sister," but I knew Gaye had nothing to do with it. Seely received one worded almost the same, except that it was signed: " Mamma and Papa." The very day they were getting back to Bisbee I saw Mrs. Herford talking through the oleander hedge with Mrs. Cash. I thought that was what they were talking about, but Mrs. Herford had the *Review* in her hands, and when the paper was back on the supper table, I could find nothing about Gaye and Miss Rudith, only an item on the front page I felt sure that Mrs. Herford had been pointing to.

Miss Anne Rolls left yesterday to make her future home with her sister, Mrs. Arthur Grafner, in Phoenix. Ill health caused her change to a lower altitude. Cochise County loses its oldest and longest established dressmaker, some of whose customers came regularly year after year from as far as Douglas and Tombstone.

We are informed that the establishment has been purchased and will be continued at the old stand over the Wheeler Assay Office.

Something in the last paragraph stirred unaccountable electricity in the back of my brain, and

when I looked through the rest of the paper, the
spark jumped. On the third page, given over mostly
to business cards that appeared week after week
without change, a new card struck my eye, standing
out boldly between that of the Opera Club, " A
Stock of Fine Liquors and Cigars," and the O.K.
Livery, Feed and Sale Stables, " Funeral Directors."

MISS TACEY CROMWELL
Fashionable Dressmaking

Main Street   Bisbee

I put down the paper, picked up my cap and
went down Main Street to see if this astounding
thing could be true. Miss Anne Rolls's name was
gone from the Wheeler Assay Building and the sign
had been changed from " Dressmaking " to " Dressmaking Parlors," but there was no indication of who
had taken it over. Occasional bright new steps had
been placed in the outside stairs that led to the
second floor. Across the street a prospector's burro
stood dozing outside the Free Silver Saloon, and
for a while I stood behind the heaped-up sacks, bed-
roll, canvas bundles, frying pans, buckets, and bulg-
ing water skins, teasing the hairless Chihuahua on
the very top, but really waiting to see if Tacey was
the actual new proprietor. After a while a team
from Kitter's warehouse hauled a long heavy yellow
table to the Wheeler Building and the men carried
it up the stairs, but they couldn't get it in the door.
Suddenly Tacey appeared on the outside second-
story landing. She was in a stylish white silk shirt-

waist and dark skirt, her hair done perfectly with a straight puff in the middle. She still looked thin, but her step was quick as it had been in the old days on Youngblood Hill, her voice clear and never hesitated. In two or three minutes she had them take off the door and the strips around it, and then the long table went in without any trouble.

If when Gaye and Miss Rudith came home that evening they knew about Tacey's move downtown, they gave not the slightest sign of it. They both looked wonderful. Miss Rudith had presents from the Islands for everyone. She gave me two marvelous spears and a bow and arrow that she said came from the head-hunters of the Philippines, and Seely went around the house that evening in a grass skirt, with a lei around her pretty neck. Before I left, the Miners' Band came up to the iron fence to serenade them. The Senator went out presently to give them some money and they played but one piece after that, a very fast and resounding one, the bass drum hardly able to keep up with the pace of the horns. Then they all hurried for Brewery Gulch and beer.

Even after Miss Rudith had me moved down from Quality Hill, I could detect no change in her equanimity. She came up herself in the carriage and Manuel carried my traps. When Mrs. Herford wiped her eyes and made believe it was a sad thing to lose me, Miss Rudith gave her a huge Chinese tapestry that she said she had bought for her on the Islands in appreciation of what she had done for me. Three or so years before, I had hated like poison to go to the Herfords'. Now I felt homesick to leave the white house on Quality Hill. The Watrous

mansion seemed a prison and when I went through
the iron gate, it clanged behind me like a barred
door. My room was in the back not far from Seely's.
I soon found that Miss Rudith and Gaye didn't
sleep in the same room like Tacey and Gaye, but
they had each their own room with a private bath-
room between. Miss Rudith had had it built before
the wedding.

Now that I lived on the same street as Tacey and
only a block or two away, I felt things were not
going well with her. Whether it was secret or out-
spoken, and what Miss Rudith had to do with it, I
never knew, but the good women of Bisbee let Tacey strictly alone. Miss Rudith brought in a dressmaker from El Paso and the former customers of
Miss Anne Rolls flocked to her.

I remember one day passing through the hall
when the Ladies' Civic League was meeting in the
sitting-room. No name was mentioned, but I knew
they were speaking of Tacey.

"Time fixes all things," Miss Rudith said quietly. "I don't think she will be here long. Mr.
Wheeler looks for her to give up her lease in November."

But November came and Tacey's sign still hung
in its accustomed place. She must have had money
put away, for she did very little sewing. I know because I went by many a time to watch. I didn't see
anyone go in or out, and I felt desperately that she
needed a friend and that I should pay her a visit.
Several times I resolved to go. I would start for the
steps firmly enough, but no steps looked so lonely
as hers, as if other feet never trod them. When I got

close I would start wondering if she'd want me to
find her alone in her dressmaking parlor with neither goods nor patterns on the long yellow table. It
might embarrass her and me too. I wouldn't know
what to say. At the last minute I would go by.

I thought surely Gaye and Seely would see what
I saw and do something for Tacey, but they were
both of a different world now. Gaye wore tall chok-
ing collars and I counted seven suits hanging in his
closet at one time. The Watrous influence had made
him vice president of the bank now and he would
take the train to Phoenix on bank business. On
one occasion he even accompanied the Senator to
Washington. He still said " tony " sometimes, and
when he laughed, his face changed in the old way
that made him look a little seedy, but his good
qualities carried him. What mattered there in those
days wasn't family, breeding, or polish. The men
who amounted to anything in the territory made
their own rude polish. They were a kind of rough
king fetched to sovereignty by their own hands.
The Senator, who, for instance, had never been a
senator except in the council of the territory, was
rugged as a bull, but mellowed to a strange tameness
with the ladies, bowing with great deference to their
wills, and so was George Druit, the capitalist, who
had once been a butcher in Brewery Gulch. I was
astonished, after I came to the mansion, how much
of Gaye's make-up fitted him to the clan.

Above everything they loved friendship and con-
viviality. I remember one time when prominent
stockholders from New York were at the dinner
table. I felt uneasy for Gaye, but I had no need to.

He sat amused at the Senator's stories of the Southwest, and when the Senator ran out, added one of
his own, about the old miner who came to the opera
house the night *Uncle Tom's Cabin* was there. Miss
Rudith corrected him that it was *Too Rich to Marry.*
He accepted the correction and went on how he
heard an old miner in front of him at the box office.
" How much downstairs? " he wanted to know.
" Dollar and a quarter," the girl said. " What's the
show? " " *Too Rich to Marry,*" she said. " Any
cheaper upstairs? " " Fifty cents in the balcony,"
she said. " What's the show up there? " " *Too Rich
to Marry,*" she said. " Anything cheaper higher up? "
" Twenty-five cents in the gallery," she said.
" What's the show up there? " " *Too Rich to
Marry,*" the girl said. " See the same show on all
three floors? " he said. " Give me a ticket half-way
up."

The stockholders laughed at this Western igno-
rance.

" I think you Easterners have that old miner
wrong," the Senator smiled. " He wasn't dumb,
just having a little fun. I know him well — Charlie
Warren. Born in New York City. Good family. He
was just trying to be entertaining."

" That reminds me," Gaye said. " They say an
old prospector came to the Copper Queen this week.
Sam, the porter, took him up to his room. The old
fellow looked a long time at the electric light. ' That's
a wonderful invention,' he said. ' Putting gas in
glass so these old desert rats can't blow it out! ' "

" That was Frank Peters," the Senator chuckled.
" He knew Tom Edison well. Was with him in that

placer job Edison had in New Mexico." He regarded the Eastern stockholders smilingly. " We're not all prairie dogs and jack rabbits out here. Lots of men and women from this territory go to Europe every summer. Lots of boys go to Harvard and Yale."

" And girls to Vassar," Gaye said, that faint smile of his directed at his wife across the table.

Then he saw me watching him and, as if I knew too much, flushed and looked away. Right then the spell was broken and he was my brother again, Seely was Seely Dowden, Brewery Gulch was just over the hill, and for a moment I could scarcely believe that the three of us were here sitting before the sparkle of glass and silver and the ruddy glow of the great copper plates above the vast sideboard.

Only Tacey seemed real, so real it didn't appear that anyone or anything could help her, not even when toward Christmas I saw a customer on her steps. It was only Mrs. Hathaway, the wife of the new mining engineer for the B. & K. who had just come to town and didn't know who Tacey was. Besides, the other dressmakers were sitting up night and day sewing for the Bisbee Social Club's New Year's ball, the big event of the year.

Seely, who was fifteen or sixteen, begged to go, but Miss Rudith said she was too young, and sent us to bed at nine. All evening the scent of Miss Rudith's bath had been drifting through the house, and after I was in bed she came in to give me goodnight, dressed in shimmering green with green slippers and jeweled buckles to match and a soft expanse of swelling bosom soft as satin and utterly without a trace of powder.

The front door had hardly closed when I heard
Seely up, and in two minutes, fully dressed, she
threw open my door.

" I'm going! " she said and I knew she meant the
ball.

" They'll bring you home," I warned her.

" I won't go in," she said. " But I'll be there."

I knew then what she had in mind and I couldn't
let her go alone. " Wait a minute," I told her.

I didn't have to tap on her door when I had
dressed. She was waiting impatiently with her coat
on and the door unlatched. The deep hall carpet
swallowed our footsteps. You could still smell Miss
Rudith's bath. Downstairs we turned the key and
slipped out the front door.

It was New Year's Eve but it wasn't cold. Although there would probably be a frost before morning, that was a long way off. There was room in the
canyon for only one other street besides Main
Street and that ran no more than a short way. Already we could hear the music, and when we got into
the alley behind the Social Club, a dark knot of
women stood there, looking up at the distant lighted
windows where couples kept passing.

" You can't see anything," I told Seely.

" You think I am going to stay here! " She scorned
me, and it sounded like the old Brewery Gulch
Seely. Then she started climbing the fence.

The women were watching us now. I was glad it
wasn't daytime, for Seely didn't care how far up she
showed her leg. Up the fence she went, then over the
sloping shed and up on the roof of the single-story
Peterson warehouse that ran front to the store. I

could hear the tin cracking under her feet, and when I got up after her, she wasn't there. Then I saw her outlined against one of the lighted windows.

The Bisbee Social Club had its own building. The first floor was luxurious with leather chairs, fine rooms for billiard tables, and a private bar. On the second floor they held their meetings and banquets and their annual ball. It was a huge room, bare ugly brick on the outside, with long narrow windows, but inside it was very fine. Although we couldn't get right against the window because of a narrow alley-way below, we were close enough to see all we wanted of the swirling mass of pinks, blues, yellows, and greens, sprinkled with the black dress suits of the men.

Now, I don't know or care much about dancing, and had come only out of compulsion, but after a little I found myself watching a lady in a red dress. Before the evening was over, Seely called it a moss rose. Its material I don't know. It looked rich and very expensive with a long heavy train. The lady that wore it was small and plumpish, not beautiful at all as I found to my surprise when I recognized her on the street later on, but there was something in that dress that made me watch her and keep looking for her. Whether from accident or design or because she was very small, she seemed to dance entirely with tall men, would lay one hand on their arm and with the other hold her long train. She didn't seem to notice where they were going, but would whirl on with her partner in perfect time. They made a picture that fascinated me, for I had never seen or imagined anything like it, the tall men and the small lady with the train of that gorgeous dress in her hand. The floor was crowded and I kept feeling they must bump or stop, but always a clear path was made for them as if like magic, or so it seemed to me.

I soon found that others watched her, too. In the intermission nearly everyone was very cordial to her and it gave me a little shock to hear Seely say:

"I wish I could dance like Mrs. Hathaway. Doesn't she have a pretty name?"

I knew then that this stunning moss-rose dress was the one that Tacey had made.

Chapter 13

SEELY

Mrs. Hathaway was the turn in Tacey's fortunes. The newcomers and some of the younger matrons began going to her for their clothes. Next fall she had carpenters put in an outside show window at the foot of her steps. After that, when you went up the boardwalk, you could always see some styled wrap, coat, or gown in it. A day or two after Virginia Harned, the wife of E. H. Sothern, had played in the opera house, there was an exact and stunning miniature of the evening dress she had worn on the stage. A card said: " Executed from Memory." I remember seeing a good many women and girls, including Seely, standing there admiring it.

In time Tacey became quite successful. Before I left Bisbee she had her own horse and rubber-tired buggy, which she kept at the O.K. Feed Stables. She never used it for business. Her customers had to come to her. It was just a symbol and recreation.

Nearly every late afternoon you could see her taking a short drive, a somber but smartly tailored figure sitting erect on her cushions, usually with the top back. She always drove alone.

Of course none of Miss Rudith's friends patronized her. The gulf between them had grown utterly fixed and unbridgeable. Tacey never recognized me any more when we met on the street. This angered me at first and didn't please even when I grew used to it and felt she did it for my own benefit. I was growing up. It had been all right for her to be a friend to a small boy. Now that I was a young man, there were complications and insinuations that she would see were left unsaid by the town. She would stiffen slightly, I thought, as we approached on the street or in the post office, yet never a glance or admission that I was there. It was different when Seely was with me. Nothing could keep Tacey's eyes off us then. They would fall on Seely and for a few seconds drink her in, intense, missing nothing. Just as we passed, they would turn to me, and such a look of dumb and piteous appeal I had never expected to see from Tacey. But what she pleaded to me for I couldn't understand then.

I was glad I didn't have her to contend with when I finished high school. The Senator and Miss Rudith wanted me to go to Lehigh, but when I put up a fight against college they said if I insisted on going to Butte and learning the mining business from the bottom as the Senator had, they would not object. Miss Rudith didn't want me to go " inside " at Bisbee. I had to do a lot of talking but secretly I was amazed that they let me have my way. I had a feeling what adamant things Tacey would have said about my going into the mines and how she would have foiled me at every turn.

That first fall and winter in Montana I grew desperately homesick for Arizona and would follow the occasional Bisbee faces I'd see on the street among the miners. I thought if I could just see Tacey or Seely, I'd be all right. Of course Tacey never wrote me a line and the most I had from Seely was an occasional picture postcard from the very select girls' school she had gone to in California. Then these stopped coming and I read to my surprise in the *Review* that Seely's friends had all been delighted to see her back in Bisbee again. A week later she was mentioned at another school.

I wondered what had happened, but the paper was very careful what it said about the leading Bisbee families. Once it had printed that a man shot for robbery in Globe was a cousin of Mrs. Ness. The next day it had apologized profusely, and from then on you had to read between the lines. Miss Rudith told me little or nothing. Her calm, affectionate letters in distinguished handwriting on green granite folders in square envelopes spoke of her progress for a Bisbee Civic Home, of Mrs. Herford's inquiries about me, and her own hopes that I was attending Church School and church. But about Seely she said nothing except to make loving and indefinite references.

Gaye scrawled me only short notes on bank stationery enclosing an occasional check, and the Senator wrote me hardly at all. There was one person who would have given me the information about

Seely. That was Matt. I think now, as I look back, he was trying to tell me all the time, but I wouldn't take it. Through the winter and spring his letters on lined tablet paper mentioned only the mines and stabbings and the latest doings in Brewery Gulch. But the following summer, when Seely was home, he kept saying where he had seen her last and what boys and men had been with her. I told myself he was only repeating talk, but a brief item in an August *Review* troubled me. It said that Miss Celia Watrous was fortunately unhurt from her harrowing experience in a runaway. No details were given, but in the following issue there was an item that Dr. Shucker had treated a certain corporal of low reputation for bruises suffered in a runaway accident with one of the Graham Livery teams.

The paper breathed no hint of connection between the two, but I instantly wondered what Seely had been doing in a livery rig with this corporal home on leave when there were always lieutenants in impeccable gauntlet gloves from Fort Huachucha. I began to remember a boy or two that Seely had been interested in when I was still at home. Now I took out and faced those names that Matt had casually but painstakingly mentioned. I remembered he had mentioned Max Houras from Chihuahua Hill, who sometimes fought in saloon bouts, and Burt Walters, a young brakeman I greatly disliked for always sitting down with women passengers and talking to them on the train, and I wondered what in God's name could be in Seely that drew her to such kind of men.

I didn't reach home for a year and a half. The fol-

lowing Christmas the Senator got me two weeks'
leave and all the way down from Montana I wondered what Seely would be like. As the train pulled
in I saw her and Miss Rudith waiting on the platform with Calvin Day. They swept to the car steps
when they saw me. Miss Rudith's delicately firm
cheek tasted as always of French toilet water. At the
time when I left, I had kissed Seely, too, but today
she made no move in that direction and neither
did I. We were both older now. She hadn't grown
taller and heavier as I had. Indeed, she looked a
trifle thinner, if anything, but her growth was there.
It had come out in other ways. Under the short
stylish jacket and the fine fur muff and neckpiece,
all worn with soft girlish ease, she was different. Her
white Irish face had fewer freckles than I remembered. But it wasn't that, nor the restless way she
looked at me and let me shake her hand. And yet it
was in all these things, something very familiar,
something that reminded me of someone, and yet
I couldn't make it out.

The Senator's big red Olds was waiting. Calvin,
who had the only garage in Bisbee, drove us home.
Most people called him Mr. Day. The Mexican
houseman carried up my bag and I went after him
to bring down the presents I had bought for Seely
and Miss Rudith. But when I came down, Seely was
gone.

"She's a young lady now, with many things on
her mind," Miss Rudith chided me gently when I
complained. "But you'll see plenty of her."

"What does she have to do? " I demanded. "Is
she trying to get Clarendon to take her back? "

" What do you mean? " Miss Rudith looked up at me.

" Well, she got kicked out of there, didn't she? " I blurted.

Miss Rudith closed the new Parker novel on her finger as she had that first day I had seen her in the hall, and today as then she had great firmness and power.

" Sit down, Nugget," she said, and when I had obeyed: " I think you have been hearing rumors, and rumors are almost never true. Perhaps Celia made one or two mistakes at the Clarendon School, but you must remember she had never been away from home before. What it was doesn't matter. She has turned over a new leaf, and as soon as she finishes at Miss Hedrick's, she is going to Vassar."

She said a great deal more in her quiet, convincing way. We must have sat there half an hour talking together, and when Seely came back she was so sweet and guileless that it shamed me. At dinner, with the electric candles shining warmly on the old copper, I saw Miss Rudith keep glancing at her with pride and affection, and once when she looked to me it was with quiet vindication. Afterward we all rose from the table together and moved down the broad hall toward the sitting-room. I expected that we would sit together and talk this first evening, but Seely halted by the door to the hall closet where our street coats and hats hung.

" Don't you want to walk around the town? " she asked me.

" At night, Celia? " Miss Rudith murmured doubtfully.

" That's the best time, Mamma. Can't we? "

"If you come back early," Miss Rudith mentioned, disappointed.

Seely did not answer directly.

" It's a wonderful evening! " She put on her toque, standing in front of the long hall glass. Then she came swiftly and kissed Miss Rudith. " Didn't you like to walk, Mamma, when you were young? "

" I hope you have a nice time." Miss Rudith's firm face had softened with loving indulgence.

Outside, Seely laid her arm on mine for a minute and every reservation I had vanished. We struck up Main Street together, Seely setting the pace and telling me how much taller and better-looking I was. I had never felt so warm and close to her, not even on Youngblood Hill. As if we were too close to let even Tacey come between us tonight, Seely did not mention her when we passed, although I saw lights in her dressmaking parlors. We passed Castle Rock and struck up Tombstone Canyon.

" Oh, I must show you off to the Herfords! " she told me suddenly as if it had just occurred to her, and when I protested, there was a soft coax of arm and breath that bribed me.

The Herfords were extravagantly glad to see us, but Seely wouldn't sit down. While we visited, she said she would run over and see Mary Harris. I should wait for her here until she came back. I noticed the Herfords were a little odd after she left, and I tried to talk them back into our first mood, but couldn't do it. Seely didn't come. I grew more and more uneasy and finally left to get Seely at the Harrises'. Before reaching the canyon there was a noise in the shadows, then swift light footsteps crossed the street, and it was Seely.

" Why didn't you wait? " she reproached me.

" Where were you? Why didn't you come? " I demanded.

" I was just coming now," she turned on me furiously. " Are you so selfish and impatient you can't even wait for me? "

Her attack silenced me, but it made me feel a little strange, and when we got back to the lighted hall at home I watched her as she told Miss Rudith what had delayed us, a spontaneous recital of truths and half-truths, all set forth with girlish animation and calling on me with such confidence to support her that I couldn't do otherwise. Whether she had been at the Harrises' or not while I was at the Herfords' bothered me. I doubted it and yet I just didn't know. I remembered that some girls couldn't stick to cold hard facts. Their recitals must be romantic, leaping from cloud to cloud. I had never thought Seely like that. Indeed, I wasn't sure now. I just knew she disturbed me and yet I felt warm and trusting toward her. More than ever she reminded me of someone tonight, but despite myself I couldn't tell who it was.

As I look back now, there was a side to Seely that won everybody. She could look at you straightforward and friendly as a little girl. Under the spirit of Christmas she was a young saint. Christmas Eve she helped the servants trim the fir on the Huachucha Mountains, and Christmas morning kissed all of us demonstratively for our presents. That night we went as a family to church to candlelight service. I

thought she was just a little different, and during
one of the carols she surprised me by bending her
head close to mine.

"Will you take me to the bullfight Saturday,
Nugget?"

It was so unexpected and her eyes had such a brilliant, restless light that I suddenly knew whom she
reminded me of. The resemblance wasn't exact, just
a combination of things seen and felt. The person
in question was someone I thought a good deal of,
perhaps more than any other in the world. And yet
the thought disquieted me. It was Tacey, the old
Tacey I had known a good while ago.

What happened from then on is something I
don't enjoy telling, even now. The border was only
a few miles from Bisbee and bullfights were an old
story, so that I couldn't understand at the time what
Seely wanted to go for. I put it down to some vagary
of her sex no man could understand. Usually these
fights were held a little earlier or later, but there
was always a parade in Bisbee, and I remember the
marching bullfighters dressed in dazzling black and
gold velvet. Zocata, whose real name was Carlos
Borrego, was in line with Vaquerita, the first ban-
derillero, and Romulus, the little Italian who wres-
tled with the bulls in the arena. He was stripped as
in the ring. As he marched along he would flex his
muscles in great knots. The Mexican band played
and all the Mexicans along the street cheered their
heroes to the sky.

I thought it curious that Seely wasn't there to see
it, but she was ready soon after Calvin brought the
automobile in front of the house. I had never seen

her eyes so brilliant. Her face and body seemed almost thin, her motions quick and restless, and yet there was such life and vitality that she almost seemed to purr. All the way down to Naco she chattered volubly, and in the box as well. Soon after the first bull was killed, she picked up her bag. " I'll be back," she said, gave me a faint little smile as she might to a trusted intimate, and left.

I supposed I knew where she was going. When a good deal of time passed and she didn't come back, I began to think I might have been mistaken and the blood and cruelty had been too much for her. After three-quarters of an hour I went out to see if she might be in the car, which had an admiring crowd of Mexicans around it, but Calvin hadn't seen her. When the fight was over and the people were pouring out, a boy I knew from School Hill came up to the car and gave me a note. It was in one of Seely's tiny envelopes. My name was on it. I tore it open. It was in her handwriting.

> Don't wait for me, Nugget. I am married.
> Celia

The time it took Calvin to drive the red car back to Bisbee would be laughed at now; but then it was a record. The great lifting finger of impenetrable dust we left behind us made that of the carriages seem thin. I heard Miss Rudith call the Senator, who at once began sending telegrams to high Mexican officials. Then Calvin drove him and Miss Rudith off in the darkness.

I endured the silent house and the whispering of the servants for a while. Later I found myself in the

hall. As I stood there putting on my coat, I knew
where I wanted to go, and when my feet approached
the Wheeler Assay office I knew this time I would
go up. It was late, but there was light still burning
on the second floor.

I can still feel myself waiting on the wooden landing after my knock, listening to that quick step my
ear knew so well.

" Nugget! " she exclaimed when she saw me. " Is
everything all right? "

I didn't want to say anything as yet. Tacey just
stood there trying to read my eyes.

" You shouldn't have come up here," she told me.

For some reason it angered me to be kept standing so long outside her door.

" You act like I'd find the wrong kind of house
up here! " I said, and instantly regretted it.

" Don't ever speak to me like that, Nugget! " she
warned in a low, intense voice. I could feel the whip-
lash across my face.

For another minute or so we stood there high over
the alleyway facing each other. I could smell Turk-
ish cigarette smoke drifting from the door.

" Will you come in? " then she invited.

I found myself in her dressmaking parlor. Its flat
tables were fairly heaped with materials and patterns. Two sewing-machines stood about and dum-
mies half covered with dresses. A cubby-hole was
hung with a long green velvet curtain. She took me
back into her parlor. It bore no resemblance at all
to her front room on Youngblood Hill. Rich gray
paper covered the walls, and there was a rug with
an encircling foot of bare polished floor in the latest

refined manner. I remember upholstered chairs and ottomans, a brass radiator, the most up-to-date horn phonograph with cylinder records, and a bamboo tabaret with a potted Christmas azalea as fine as any Miss Rudith had in the house. Along the wall was a glassed-in bookcase with piles of women's and foreign fashion journals. In the row of books I thought I could still make out the orange cloth of the *English Speaker* and the red paper cover of *The Ladies' Companion*.

" Why, this is grand, Tacey! " I stammered.

She gave me a cool look as if to ask what I had expected her place to be like. At the same time, I think, it pleased her.

" Would you like to see it, Nugget? " she asked, more friendly, but watching me. " This is my little dining-room." Her hand turned on the flood of colored electric light from a hanging dome of stained glass. A pale blue rug lay on the floor and the wallpaper had a frieze of colored foreign scenes. Table, buffet, and chairs were in the latest fumed-oak Eastern style, and framed prints of fruit and game hung on the walls.

" There's just room to stick your head in my kitchen," she said, and pulled on the light. I remember it as a very daring light gray with a refrigerator such as they advertised in the window of the company store painted to match. She did not offer to show me her bath or bedroom, but I had a glimpse through the open door of a yellow silken spread worked with her own stylish monogram, and dressing-table with a tall mirror that I would have sworn held tucked-in pictures of Seely and me.

" Is it as nice as you expected? " she asked lightly, but I felt the sensitive pause and danger.

" I expected it would be nice, Tacey," I told her. " But this is a whole lot nicer."

I saw her relax, but only for a moment. When we sat down in her little parlor, the question why I had come rose again in her eyes. I took out a cigarette and offered her one, but she didn't like that and refused it.

" Is Gaye all right? " she asked.

" I guess so," I said. " If he didn't do another tap he wouldn't need to worry."

" Don't ever tell him that! " Tacey admonished me. She was silent awhile and then she spoke. I was astonished at her passion. " He should go into politics. He could be treasurer of Arizona if he wanted to. Everybody likes him. The miners and the mine-owners would vote for him. The gamblers and the saloon men, too."

" Arizona's still a territory," I reminded her. " Everybody's appointed."

" It'll be a state soon! " she flashed. " Even now he could get out a petition. Everybody would sign it. The Governor would have to pay attention then."

" Yes, he could do that," I said eying her.

" But don't say I said so," Tacey said quickly. " Remember, you thought of it yourself." She sat quietly for a time now, although I could feel her watching me. In the end I could stand it no longer.

" It's Seely, Tacey! " I told her, and saw the fear that had been far back in her eyes ever since I came fly into her face.

" What happened? " she asked, and when I told her, she just stared at me, very white.

" We don't even know yet who it is," I told her.

" How in God's name can you live with her and be so blind! " she lashed. " All of you, I mean! "

" I think it'll be all right," I tried to defend myself. " I heard Miss Rudith say they were bringing her back. They're annulling it. Everything's going to be just like before."

Tacey regarded me with tortured pity.

" You think it was any good before? " she asked, wetting her lips.

" You seem to know more about it than I do," I said sullenly. " If you know, why don't you tell me? "

Tacey sat for a long time.

" All I know, Nugget," she said at last, " is something you wouldn't understand. And I couldn't tell you if you did. I couldn't tell anybody. It isn't about Seely exactly. It's about somebody else, somebody I once knew very well. Perhaps it's too late now anyway. I just don't want to say any more." She was silent a little. " I appreciate your coming, Nugget, and I'm not saying this for you to go. But when you do, please don't come up here any more."

Chapter 14

THE GOOD WOMEN

Montana was cold with snow when I got back, and fogged with a dampness we never knew in the Mule Mountains. Any day I'd have given my dinner for a look at the sun. But the only sun I got was second-hand in the Bisbee *Review,* and in Matt's and Miss Rudith's letters. I had hoped that after my visit I might hear something from Tacey. I could remember her handwriting from Youngblood Hill, a straight up-and-down hand, sometimes a backhand, always with a very fine pen. When no letter came I told myself she didn't want her misspelled words criticized. But inside I knew she'd never write to me.

I wanted to hear about Seely. Of course I knew, and we all knew now, that she had married Tom Ferrebee, who had been in her class at school, a slim, dark-haired boy, a good dresser and always with the girls. His father was dead and his mother had a small notion store. I never saw him in Bisbee again and suspected that the Senator paid him to stay away.

Matt never wrote of Seely any more. He wrote about the rusty old Winchester dug up on O.K. Street, the new eight-hour shifts at the mines, and the victims of the black-heart plague, whose lungs and other organs turned black as coal. Miss Rudith didn't mention these things. Her letters had become fewer and shorter. She told of the church, of the Senator, but scarcely a word of Seely. The last I saw her name was when the *Review* printed a front-page account of Mrs. Jarley's Waxworks. It was something put on by the Episcopal Women's Guild. I remember there were the Queen of Sheba and Susan B. Anthony among others. Seely was Joan of Arc. The *Review* said George Dunninger had brought Joan of Arc out on the stage on the baggage truck, taking a feather duster out of his hip pocket, dusted her off, face and all, and she had never turned an eyelash. That was Seely to a T. Some of the Cornishmen swore she was a real figure of wax. But I thought it strange that no line about Mrs. Jarley's Waxworks had come from Miss Rudith.

Not till I came back the following fall did I learn that the night of the show Seely had run off with Max Houras, a barber in the City Shop. For a week Miss Rudith had officers searching, but this time the law failed to find them. Most people thought they had gone to Mexico City. A good while later when a letter came, it was postmarked Cripple Creek. Seely wrote that she was happy and that Max had a job. What Miss Rudith wrote her no one ever knew. Perita told me she had seen her write out a check for a hundred dollars, but when she took the letter over to the post office it was so light it couldn't have held more than a few lines.

I was shocked when I saw Miss Rudith in October. She didn't come to the station, but met me in her front sitting-room with the shades of the windows drawn. Still she couldn't hide the heavy gray streak in her hair. For the first time since I knew her she looked like the Senator. That was handsome enough for an old mining man, but on Miss Rudith the effect was tragic.

She rose when I came in, and held me hard against her, never saying a word. It was like the first meeting after a shocking death in the family. We sat together in the sitting-room and she asked about my work, the Montana country, and the people she knew around Butte. But all the time I could tell it was a great effort. I noticed the servants watched her intently as they moved quietly about the big house. Seely's name was never mentioned. Yet walking to the church by her side, where Seely had always walked, and kneeling beside her on the prayer stool where Seely had knelt before, and hearing in my ears her impassioned sibilants in the responses, the Apostles' Creed and the Lord's Prayer, I felt that it would have been much easier on her if she had said it.

There was something Sunday morning about Miss Rudith in the hall, hatted and gloved for church, that filled me with dread. All the way up the hill she moved silently, almost majestically, but you could feel the bitterness within. As we approached the church door, her head would go up as if braving a multitude, and her face become granite. Even her church dresses of rich black and white silk and of purple taffeta had something unyielding about them, as if the point in the front of each bodice was of iron.

All these years I knew that Tacey had been coming to church although she had never tried to join it. The Watrous pew stood in the front, while Tacey chose her seat far to the rear. She was always gone when we came to leave. But if she happened to be already there when we came in and especially if she sat along the aisle, I could feel Miss Rudith draw up and stiffen. It was only Tacey's slender back and smart hat that she had to pass. Ahead to look at was the altar with its initialed cloths, fresh flowers, and burning white candles. And yet for a little there was such a polarity between them, such a clashing of unseen forces, that I could feel it long after we reached our pew.

What Miss Rudith thought or felt was her own secret, and she wasn't the one to confide any more than a planet moving firmly and inexorably in its course. But she must have suffered a very deep humiliation in front of everyone, and a conviction that Tacey's early influence was to blame. Even so I was startled to learn that she had bought the Wheeler Building and meant to tear it down and erect her long-cherished Civic Home. The transaction was secret and not to take effect or be recorded until the middle of November. Tacey's lease would have expired then and the possibility of hurting Gaye's political chances this fall would be over. Yet I couldn't quite feel that it was meanness on Miss Rudith's part. Miss Rudith was never mean. It must be, I told myself, a righteous impulse to purge Bisbee of that contaminated second floor on Main Street and to put a wholesome town charity in its stead.

Gaye was friendlier this time than I had ever known him, and livelier. Since summer he had been out for territory treasurer. I knew from the *Review* that long lists of signers in Bisbee, Globe, and other mining centers had petitioned the governor with his name. He claimed to have no hopes of getting it, but thrived on the attention and excitement and the jocular pleasantries of the men. He surprised me by asking how I was fixed for money and dropped a gold eagle in my pocket. " Keep your eye open for bad five-dollar pieces, boy," he said. " A lot of them around. Nick them with your knife. If they're counterfeit you'll strike silver."

There are times when I have wondered at our inability to read the future. Looking back, some signs are plain enough. For example, July and August had been very wet in Bisbee that year. I had read in the *Review* that the flood-gates by the Roundly-Larson store had to be closed nearly every day. The water had come down Tombstone Canyon four feet deep against the gates. Every few days the *Review* had been full of it.

Doctor Swingle, the hair specialist, had tried to cross Main Street in front of the Opera Club and the miners had had to pull him out. The tin cans and boxes, outhouses and hookers' cribs that came down Brewery Gulch had no end. Burros and men had been swept helpless down the red current and only half of them were lucky enough to be fished out at the big culvert. Most everybody had his steps roped to the houses and, according to the *Review*, the last seen of Humphrey's milk wagon was when it sailed past Lowell in the flood. Most every evening after the water was down, men had had to clear away mud and debris packed three feet deep against the flood-gates. The next day might dawn fine and clear, but by afternoon everybody had to scurry to his own side of the street before it was too late.

Millions of gallons of water had flowed to waste down Naco Road that summer and at the end of a dry September the people up School Hill and other high spots began complaining as usual of the lack of it. The town had grown too fast and had no water system as yet worthy of the name. By October when I came the situation was still worse and I remember passing the Copper Queen Hotel and hearing guests call down that they had no water.

If we were ever short, Miss Rudith never complained. She put nearly her whole time now on plans for her new Civic Home. Gaye knew what was going to happen to the Wheeler Assay Building, of course, and I would see him grow uncomfortable when she showed him the architect's sketches. At such times Miss Rudith's haggard face calmed and strengthened, and when she came home from the ordeal of church, there was a victorious power about her, something that seemed to say: " The mills of God grind slowly, but they grind exceeding small."

I remember it was the day the Governor announced his choice for the offices of territory. The *Review* the day before had said that he had asked for the resignation of all the leftovers from the last administration. Today the *Review* printed his new appointments. Every office was named except that of treasurer. When I went down to the depot, Al Carnes, the agent, asked me as he stamped and pounded my dangling ribbon ticket for Montana if Gaye wasn't going to get it. I told him that no news had come in as yet, but when I got back to the house I thought it had, and that it was bad. I saw the Senator come out of the sitting-room, where he had been talking to Miss Rudith. I knew by his walk that something grave had happened. When I looked in the sitting-room door, Miss Rudith's face was white and shaken.

I started in, but the Senator called me and took me behind the banister.

"There's nothing you can do, Nugget," he said deep in his throat. "That damned woman was here telling her things about Seely."

"What?" I wanted to know.

"It's just rumor. I'd pay no attention to it or Mrs. Ness either."

"Is Seely dead?" I persisted.

"No." The Senator lowered his grizzled, bull-like head. "I don't like to say this. But it might have been better for Rudith if she was." He tightened his mouth and took several stiff breaths. "She's just going to hell the fastest way she knows how."

I knew he meant Seely and I felt my face pale like Miss Rudith's.

"Can't we do anything?" I wondered.

"Nobody can do anything. If it's in the blood, it's got to come out. She had a baby. It was born dead.

Since then she's lit out. Nobody knows where she is, but that damn woman claims she knows somebody who saw her running and singing in dance halls."

"Have you said anything to Max Houras?" I stammered.

"She's left him." The Senator looked grim. "Not nineteen years old yet, and already she's had two men! God knows how many more." He stood there strong and bull-like, but the skin of his face was old and mottled and I saw his hand tremble. When I looked up, Miss Rudith had come silently out in the hall and was climbing the stairs to her room.

When I got out of the house I went up to Matt's place to give him good-by. He was working now in the Lowell shaft, drilling rounds like a man. He didn't go on till the graveyard shift, and we walked up to O.K. Street together. We had passed the Pythian Castle when a Mexican on Chihuahua Hill ran out of his shack and fired a shotgun twice in the air. From where I was I could see no reason for it, nor could Matt. There was smoke hanging high above Main Street, but the yellow sulphur from the smelter always hung there when the wind blew up the canyon. After a while we heard the tap of the fire-bell.

Still we didn't hurry. We had seen firemen run before, Gaye with the others. A hose race on the Fourth of July was getting to be the rage lately. Last summer teams from Naco, Douglas, and Tombstone had fought with Bisbee for the shining copper cup. It was something to see them sprint, dragging their carts a hundred and fifty feet while some kept jumping off to pull down the hose till all three lengths were out. The trick was to get the plugs screwed on at one end and the nozzles at the other. If water came out before the nozzle was fast, it was no go. The Company that made the best time under the stop watches got the prize. They always had a crowd, a good deal of beer, and, when someone got wet, plenty of gibes and laughter.

But no such sound greeted us when we got down to Main Street today. A silent crowd stood in the canyon watching a three-story brick rooming house called the Philadelphia Hotel stand wrapped in flames and smoke. They had the hoses playing on it by the time we got there, and after a little you could see the fire sink gradually lower as if the valves of a great oil stove were being slowly turned down.

I had no idea then, nor had anybody else, that we were looking at something that would be talked of in Arizona for forty years to come. The dark smoke drifting up Tombstone Canyon grew noticeably less dense. The crowd began to limber up, spread itself, and to talk, all symptoms that the worst was over. I shook hands good-by with Matt and went back toward the house.

Before I reached the final bend in Main Street a hue and cry rose behind me. When I looked around, the firemen were still holding their brass nozzles pointed toward the fire, but no water came out. They yelled to the men at the plugs angrily. The latter bent and worked over their plugs with a kind of frantic futility. As I stood there watching, yellow and black smoke edged with red began to boil slowly out of the building again. Firemen stared at it half paralyzed. The wind drawing up the canyon pulled at my hat. How great a draft it made through those blackened gaps of doors and windows I could only guess. Till I got there I could hear the timbers, floors, and plaster crackling and fusing like the wood, coke, lime, and ore in a flowing smelter. Suddenly the firemen broke and ran, bawling at one another. Now I could see it, too — sparks spouting like a vast pot of fireworks from the roof of the Quigley Building next door.

By the time I had worked my way through the crowd to find Matt again, the Philadelphia Hotel and the Quigley Building were welded as one. Red heat glared from lower storerooms where men were wont to drink over a bar or recline in barber chairs. Already they were throwing bolts of cloth from the doors and windows of the adjoining Bon Ton Store and soon great unwinding bolts of smoke followed. Sparks were driving now before the draft in livid showers, and waves of elastic flames rolled and licked around the fronts and cornices of the Hoffman House, the Jensen Block with its hardware and cash stores, the Mills Building and its National Tea Company, the Johns lock and repair shop, and the barn and sheds of the Palace Livery Stable.

How quickly it happened is difficult to tell afterward and tell it true. Time of excitement is different from other time, and no man I saw thought to look at his watch. Certain it is that the time it took was miraculously short. Since then I have heard recitals of other conflagrations in Colorado mining towns, and the pitiful stories are much the same. The towns are built in steep narrow canyons. Here,

like the pit of a furnace, the draft draws and the
heat is held till it goes through the walls as though
they were paper. As the canyon rises, one building
stands above another, overlapping it like fresh dried
fuel piled higher and higher to burn, so that once
fire starts, nothing but the Lord God in heaven can
stop it.

In an hour or two all Main Street was sending
up black clouds and they had begun to empty the
mines. With every lift miners were pouring out to
help fight the common foe. Men who had gone
through the San Francisco fire pleaded with own-
ers to dynamite their buildings, but when permis-
sion was given, it was too late. At dark the electric
lights went suddenly off, leaving only the lurid glare.
By the red lights you could see merchants farther
up the canyon hurriedly piling stock out in the
street, and wagons and men carrying it away. The
Elks' Building stood off the attack for a while, giving rise to hope, but soon it was roaring away with
the rest. Gradually the heat in the clinker pit of the
canyon grew so great it jumped the street, fired the
Trumbull Building, and both sides of the street
started racing up the canyon together.

Fire now was spreading in every direction. From
where I stood I could see it running up steep Clawson Hill, licking up rooming and private houses and
lighting up all the frightened faces. The thunder
of dynamite roared above the crackle of the flames.
You could hear it run along the crest of the hills
above, where crowds of watchers from Bisbee, Warren, and Lowell lined the cliffs. They told me afterward that standing up there was like looking down

in the pit of hell. People whose houses stood in the path of the flame fled to higher ground carrying their most valuable possessions. Everybody worked including myself. I saw the Senator, his great face and gray suit black with char and sweat, piling provisions from Murphy's store out in the street. Little Pat Murphy, drawn with panic, never knew what he was doing. " Here! " he'd yell from the doorway at the Senator as if he were a mule and the Senator would obediently trot up the steps, shift a barrel to his broad back, and carry it out to the middle of the street.

I saw the Douglases doing good deeds that night and Colonel Brown, too. They took a five-year-old Finnish boy sick with smallpox down from the third floor of the Hoffman House and nobody thought to avoid him. I hardly stopped to watch when Riggs, the plumber, jumped into a blanket from the roof of the Opera Club. But to see houses that had sheltered people I knew swept away almost instantly in smoke did something to my stomach. I watched old Granny Darwill, who had slaved her entire life, standing staring while all she owned was destroyed in a few minutes, her arms piled with only worthless things she had saved. People went crazy with the blind instinct to save. I could see the rim of the hills piled with goods of every description. Men and women stood guard over them with rifles and shotguns.

People said now that all of Bisbee would go. Naco Road, School Hill, Opera Drive, Brewery Gulch, and Chihuahua Hill, each was doomed. It seemed impossible to think that all this had started from a small trash fire in a closet of the Philadelphia Hotel. Tommy Blair said there was a time when if he but had a hose he could have put it out himself.

Only when things stood at their darkest did the tide turn. Up the canyon the natural barriers at Castle Rock stopped the long sweep. Back down the canyon the walls of the Henninger Building stood like a fortress against the terrific heat of the Martin Block and so did the thick barricade of Hillary brick on the south side. How the men who lined the roofs endured the heat while they poured down sand and beat out sparks I don't know. But those miners could stand anything. A great number of them, including picked dynamiters, kept School Hill only scorched and scarred.

As soon as the flames were under control, Main Street was jammed again with excited people. Some were drunk, many fighting. Police swore in scores of deputies and closed what saloons hadn't been burned out. I saw men hunting wives, and wives seeking husbands, and both after missing children. On every side you could hear reunions of friends as if they hadn't seen each other for years. Those that still had houses or cabins offered their roofs to the homeless. " You can stay with us," must have been said a great many times that night.

I met Gaye pushing down through the crowd. He looked almost cool and untouched. Scarcely a hair was laid back on him. But when we got down away from the fire I noticed he smelled rank with charred plaster and pine like the rest of us.

" How is it up the canyon? " I asked, meaning the Wheeler Building.

"All gone," he said briefly and started on. I had
to hurry to keep up with him.

"They say it'll cost the town a million!" I chattered.

"That's a little high."

"There's a hundred places burned!" I told him.

"I think you're still a little high, Nugget," he
said.

I thought he was on his way back to the house,
but he turned in at the bank, which was unburned
and unlocked. Far back in the directors' room I had
a glimpse of men huddled around the table with
lighted candles. I didn't know then, but everybody
found out later that here in this back room that night
the town was rebuilt even before the special relief
trains had started from Phoenix.

Gaye stood there a moment with the door open
before he went in. He seemed to see somebody down
the street, and when I looked I saw it was Miss Rudith. The electric lights were still off, but acres of
embers lighted up everything in an unearthly red
glow. Miss Rudith was bareheaded and coming this
way, in her older black coat with the Persian-lamb
collar she wore now only to the mountains or desert.
I thought she was going to ask me about Gaye, who
by this time had gone into the bank, but she went
right by although so close that I could see the wide
gray streak in her hair. She paid no attention as I
followed, either to me, to the smoldering and hiss-
ing ruins on either side, or to the fallen brick walls
and piles of dynamited debris she had to climb over.
After she had passed the second or third bend I saw
her pause and look around. She might have been a

sleepwalker coming to herself and trying to find out where she was. I knew how she felt. It was like coming back to a vanished town that you once knew as well as your hand, but now you couldn't even tell where your mother's door had stood. All the landmarks were gone. Surely these charred and smoking shambles with wrecked walls and blackened brick and stone had been nothing you had laid eyes on before.

She moved a little farther up the canyon and turned an object on the ground under her foot. It looked like a human head. Then something in me contracted as I recognized it as part of a dummy that I had seen standing in Tacey's room. I think Miss Rudith had recognized it, too. She peered at the empty unfamiliar space on that side of the street. A building had once stood here. It was gone now, but there was still part of a foundation wall remaining with chunks of green copper ore mortared around the vanished doorstep. This must have been the building she had bought to tear down and put up her Civic Home in its place. It had not been burned. Everything testified to the fearful hurry in which the dynamiters had blasted it out of the way.

Behind the wall were the battered ruins of several assay furnaces. A motionless figure stood there with what looked like the crumpled horn of a phonograph in her hand. Now the woman bent and picked up something. I couldn't see very well but it turned out later to be a ragged and worthless piece of cloth.

The woman came out with her souvenirs, and Miss Rudith gave a start as she saw it was Tacey. For a long moment they again faced each other here not over a block from where they had seen each other the first time.

I didn't know whether, even under the common leavening of the fire, they would speak or not. And if they did, I thought, it would be a great deal for Miss Rudith just to murmur a few formal words about the damage and destruction. Certainly it shows how little I knew about women and about Miss Rudith and Tacey in particular. I think now that they could have been faced on all sides by the living fire at this time and yet when they saw each other, there could have been but one subject in their minds.

" Miss Cromwell! " I heard Miss Rudith in an unexpected low, woman's cry. " Did you know about Seely and her baby? "

Tacey looked at her.

" Yes," she said harshly. " I know."

" The baby is dead! " Miss Rudith told her with anguish.

" Yes, I've heard," Tacey said. This time her voice shook a little, and I think it must have been this faint trembling that misled Miss Rudith.

" Did you know," she faltered, " what she is doing — singing in saloons? "

" What's that to me? " Tacey flew at her. " I'm not her mother."

Miss Rudith had drawn back sharply.

" I didn't mean — " she began stiffly and confused, but the bars in Tacey's brain were down now and the pent-up harvest of years was pouring out. Her eyes were green metallic fire.

" You're her mother, but you want me to suffer.

I won't suffer. I'm not responsible. Nine years ago you took her away. I wasn't fit — I wasn't decent to have a child around me. You brought her up your own way. Fine things and a fine mansion and never a look at me! Well, I hope you're satisfied. Maybe it works with saints and decent people. But I want to tell you there are kids who have the devil and all hell to fight in themselves. Oh, it's easier on you to pet and spoil them and believe all they say and let them go their own way. It saves a lot of hard talk and nasty watching and uglier thinking. But I want to tell you that if there is a Christ, it's one who knows what sinners are and how they'll go straight to hell if He doesn't watch out and hold them up at every danger. Maybe such a kid likes you when you let him do anything he wants to. But later if he goes bad, I tell you he'll hate and curse you — "

" Please — stop! " Miss Rudith begged her. She was standing there white, stricken, and swaying. I hurried, but Tacey got to her first.

" I'm sorry, Mrs. Oldaker," she said simply.

" I'm sorry, too," Miss Rudith whispered. She tried to say something of Seely, but the name almost seemed to choke her and in a moment both women were weeping, holding fast to each other's hands and letting out some of their common misery and grief. Only an untrodden gulf between them, I believe, kept them from each other's arms.

" You have no place to sleep," Miss Rudith said suddenly in a strong firm voice, loosening her hands and wiping her eyes. " You must come down and stay with us tonight."

Chapter 15

THE SUMMIT

I POKED around for a time before going down the
the canyon. Most of the way I expected to meet
Tacey's swift step returning. But when I reached
the mansion's front door, something in the face of
Perita, the Mexican maid, warned me what to expect and as I came in I found Tacey in the parlor
with politicians who were waiting for Gaye and, in
a corner, the weary, red-eyed Parkers, who had been
burned out on Clawson Hill.

The electric lights had not yet come on and the
great room looked deep and cavernous with lighted
oil lamps and candles. For Tacey's sake I was glad
for the dimness. Up in the canyon she had been her
swift, intense, unashamed self. Here alone on a huge
sofa, with the grand piano and the gold and marble
tables around her, she had stiffened and changed.
She looked ill at ease, on the defensive, as I had

scarcely seen her of late. Her eyes met mine with veiled defiance. There was a look in them that she had come against her better judgment. She hadn't taken off her coat. Miss Rudith, still haggard, tried to do the right thing to her in front of all. But each time she turned to speak to her, I thought with a sinking heart that Tacey showed herself at her worst.

The men sat around silent and uncomfortable. The Mayor was there and Burt Welsh, territory legislator from Bisbee; Cyrus Dull, a famous mining lawyer; Jax Bilheim, who ruled Lowell, Warren, and Brewery Gulch with an iron hand; and others. Mr. Dull was telling about election nights in Colorado he recalled, with shooting and flambeau squads. At the word from their leader, he said, the torch men would put their mouths to their mouthpieces and blow, and the flames would leap up four or five feet in unison. It was a sight to see. The shotgun squad was more of a nuisance. Their leader would call: "Ready! Aim! One! Two!" and they would fire first one barrel and then the other. It made a terrific racket in the streets.

I saw that the men in the room were much relieved when the Senator came down. He had bathed his face and hands with water we always kept in reserve, and had changed. Now in his courteous way, with mustaches flowing, he bowed to Tacey, among others, as if he had not passed her a thousand times on the street without a glance.

"Gaye not back yet?" he asked. "He's to call Central when he gets in."

I thought I saw a faint fire in Tacey's eyes.

"The exchange closes at ten, doesn't it?" Mrs. Parker put in.

"Not tonight," the Senator said heartily.

Gaye's step sounded on the porch a little later. I can still see him standing in the parlor doorway as his eyes found Tacey sitting there. You couldn't say that his face altered any more than it used to over a big play at his faro table. His brown mustache kept casually drooping. His left eye, always a trifle more pointed than the right, suffered no further change. And yet something happened to the parlor the moment he came into it, a distinct, suppressed livening. A moment ago, with Miss Rudith neutralized, there had been only one pole in the room, a negative one. Now positive and negative poles had been brought within thirty feet of each other, and though Gaye did not look at Tacey again you could feel the electric tension generated between them. It stirred up even the fire-weary politicians. I could feel faint prickles in my scalp and fingers.

"Central wants you, dear," Miss Rudith said, and at the last word I felt the two poles secretly quiver.

I expected Gaye to back out of the parlor with considerable relief, but he coolly continued to stand there for a while, telling the story of how Alec Maddox had dynamited the house of his enemy, Leo Phelan, out of the path of the flames. Then as if refusing to admit Tacey's presence, he went, matter-of-fact, no farther than to the wall telephone in the hall.

As a rule during another's telephone call, men talked politely in low tones to show that they weren't listening. But tonight even the conversation on who

had insurance and who hadn't quickly petered out
and died.

"Hello, hello!" we could hear Gaye say time
after time and I felt sure the call came from a far-
away place like Phoenix. Then of a sudden he said a
different kind of hello, and you knew at once that
he could hear and somebody was there. He talked
a long time, first about the fire then about the relief
trains.

"No, no!" he said briefly at the end. "Absolutely nothing's come in here. The Governor must
have named someone else." And he hung up.

There was a long uneasy silence when he came
back. The men's strong faces looked disappointed,
and in my own mind the Governor's desk in Phoenix
with the copper statuette of Teddy that they said he
always kept on top had grown suddenly dim and
far away. Only Tacey seemed undiscouraged. She
had even straightened a little and fighting red spots
burned in her cheeks.

By ones and twos the politicians left, and the
Senator busied himself answering wires that had
come about his and the family's safety during the
fire. Miss Rudith showed the weary Parkers to bed,
and I was ready to go myself when the telephone
rang again. The Senator answered it. We heard him
say: "Yes," several times in that clipped, casual,
reflective way he had when it didn't mean anything;
then: "Send it over," he said briefly and hung up.
His huge powerful face and sweeping mustache gave
no indication of any emotion when he returned. He
glanced around the room. Gaye was back in what
we called "the office," and there was left in the

big parlor only myself and Miss Rudith, who was trying to induce Tacey to go upstairs to bed.

"Let's have some coffee and sandwiches first," the Senator said.

Perita and a sleepy Josefa brought in the great silver tray and even Gaye had come reluctantly up the hall when the doorbell rang.

"Bring him in," the Senator said offhand to Perita, his mouth full of sliced tongue. He thrust his great nose in a coffee cup and kept it there till the maid appeared with the boy, a limp envelope in his hand. "He looks tired," the Senator said. "Give him a sandwich and a cup of coffee."

The boy looked slightly bewildered that no one took his message. You could see a dance in the Senator's old eyes and you knew he was holding something off as long as he could.

"You're working late tonight, son," he mentioned.

"Yes, sir," the boy stammered, his eyes on the great silver urn now being tapped for his coffee. "Too many people sending telegrams. They want to know if everybody else is all right. We got more telegrams and answers now than we can send till daylight."

"They must have heard of our fire."

"Why, they've seen it as far as Globe!" the boy cried. "Over two hundred miles."

When Perita handed him his sandwich and coffee the message fell to the floor.

"That looks like a telegram, boy!" the Senator said with mock severity. He picked it up. "What do you mean not delivering it?"

The boy crammed in the sandwich as if it might
be taken away.

" Here." The Senator gave him a silver dollar and
held the message out to Gaye. " It's for you."

I shot a look at Tacey, then back to Gaye. He
must have known that all this dignified horseplay
was for something. But his mouth under that brown
hayrake of a mustache was unchanged. His finger
quietly forced back the flap of the scarcely pasted
envelope. Stepping over to a candle he glanced down
the long handwritten sheet. Only a pushing out of
his mustache showed his emotion.

" Will you read it, sir," he asked the Senator.

The latter fetched out his glasses. They were of
horn or strong tortoise shell and rode the middle of
his nose. He leaned back his head to focus through
them.

" Phoenix! " he read aloud, then threw his great
head forward to glance over the glasses significantly
around the room.

But our eyes, I think, were on Gaye. He stood
there in his quiet nerveless way and what his
thoughts were nobody knew. I remembered the first
time I had seen him, in his loud checkered suit behind the White Palace roulette wheel. It seemed
strange that I didn't feel him my brother then.
That's when he seemed like my brother, I thought
now; then and that first night in Bisbee hanging
back and letting Tacey go ahead and do the register-
ing in the dim little Brewery Gulch hotel. I could
see him again months later sitting in our cabin on
Youngblood Hill over a worn faro layout and, when
pleased, drawing a hand over the two piles of chips,

leaving them a single red and white stack like a thick stick of peppermint candy. All that seemed ages ago now.

The Senator's voice, reading the telegram, came resoundingly through my thought.

" ' To the Hon. Gaye Oldaker, Bisbee, Arizona. A vacancy having occurred in the office of territorial treasurer, I hereby appoint you said treasurer of the territory of Arizona, to be effective on the first day of November next. On presentation of this telegram to the secretary of the territory, commission will be issued you and this telegram may be taken as authority for same.' " The Senator's voice shook faintly. " It's signed by the Governor," he said.

Indeed, it was suddenly like presidential election evening when a magic lantern threw the returns on a big sheet across from the *Review* building — or like the night of the Jeffries-Fitzsimmons fight when the Empire Saloon had a direct wire from the ringside, with a telegraph key clicking through the heavy cigar haze, with the latest returns read aloud by Fred Downey in a full-dress suit and all the games running full tilt and bigger bets than usual stimulated by the excitement.

I glanced at Tacey. Her stiffness and defensive air had left her. She sat there with head lifted, a small, slight person, but generating such intensity that she dominated the great sofa, pushed it firmly into the background, made it only her setting. The wings of the imperious carved eagle seemed to hover over her approvingly now. I watched her but she never saw me. Her look on Gaye literally bathed him with blinding green triumph.

The Senator still stood with the telegram hanging from his hand, looking down over his glasses, pleased with the scene.

" How about some wine, Perita? " he called; then his huge fist rummaged in his pocket for a key and gave it to Miss Rudith, who left for the cellar with Perita. I hurried after. The truth was I didn't want to be left behind with Tacey and Gaye, whose position would be a hard and embarrassing one now.

When I came back fortified by Miss Rudith and the Senator's sparkling burgundy, the great parlor sofa with its high carved eagle was empty. Tacey had taken her fortune at its crest and gone. None whom Miss Rudith questioned claimed to have seen her go, and it was a long time afterward before I learned where she had slept that night.

Chapter 16

OVER THE HILL

I DID not see Bisbee again for nearly three years. I was underground when the word came. Mr. Reilly himself brought down the telegram of Miss Rudith's death. The next morning I was on the train.

It wasn't altogether unexpected. The first summer after the fire her car had broken down in the mud half-way to the New Mexican line. The road wasn't more than wheel tracks then and they had been out twenty-four hours in the rain before a buckboard from the nearest ranch reached her. The *Review* printed a long account of it and always afterward in telling of her ill health used the phrase: " since her accident," which seemed strange to me. The Senator had been with her and even at his age hadn't suffered. But Miss Rudith had gone back to Bisbee ill, Doctor Shucker had put her to bed, and from that time on she had seldom left her room. Indeed,

this was chiefly why I hadn't been home in such a
long time. With Seely gone and the new heavy
silence and gloom of Miss Rudith's illness, the big
house repelled me. I wouldn't have known what to
do or say. Also I felt sure that it wasn't the " automobile accident " but Seely that Miss Rudith suffered from, and if it hadn't been that, something
else would have had to be blamed.

It was early September the day I got the telegram,
and that morning in Butte we had waked up to our
first fall of snow. All the way down, the mountains
were white, and the air when I stepped out of the
train cold and raw. It seemed like a brighter and
kindlier world down in Arizona and I couldn't believe that anyone so strong and with as much to live
for could die in this soft air, blue sky, and warm
sunshine. My train came in about eleven Sunday
morning. Calvin was waiting for me and rushed me
up to the church where the funeral was being held
instead of the regular morning service.

" Has everyone else come, Calvin? " I asked.

" I think so, Nugget," he said.

" Who's here? " I wanted to know.

" Well, there's a lot I don't know from Phoenix.
But the Cardwells and Bargers from Cananea — "

" I mean the family," I interrupted.

" Oh, yes. Most of her people came."

" Nobody else? " I persisted.

Calvin seemed a little uncomfortable.

" Well, they say Miss Celia came last evening.
I didn't see her myself. She's not at the house."

As we approached the church I could see many
women from Brewery Gulch and the hills standing

outside, and as I stepped down I heard that the services had already begun. The church was crowded as I had almost never seen it, but Fred Langer was waiting at the door and ushered me at once up the aisle to the front pew where the family sat. The Senator, looking much older than I ever remembered him, squeezed my arm feelingly as he rose and stepped out to let me in. But Gaye next to him gave me only a quiet look of recognition as he moved over to make me room. I glanced beyond him as I pushed in, but the people next to him were Miss Rudith's cousins and uncle from the East.

All I remember of the service is the heavy, blanketing scent of flowers in the church and what Calvin had said of Seely. I kept wondering where in the church she might be sitting and how much I would find her changed. Once or twice I managed a surreptitious glance around in the hope of seeing her, but all I found were strange eyes staring at me. In the end we sat quiet while the others filed out pew by pew for a last look at Miss Rudith. Everybody was in the carriages by then, but I turned back while Fred Langer and his assistant were fastening the lid.

" Did Miss Celia view the body? " I stammered.

He gave me a grave and uneasy look.

" She wasn't in the church, Nugget," he said in a very low voice.

I remembered then what Miss Rudith herself had once said — that rumors were nearly always false — and I decided that Seely wasn't in town at all. Indeed, it was very doubtful if she would show her face here again. But in the cemetery at Lowell, while

Brother John conducted the service at the grave, I
thought I heard an untoward sound. It startled me,
for none of us showed our grief. I was standing between the Senator and Gaye. Neither one gave notice that he had heard, but when I turned my head,
I saw Seely. I am not sure that I would have known
her if Tacey hadn't been with her. They stood away
from everyone, by themselves, as if they hadn't the
same right there as the rest of the mourners, but
were resolved not to stay away. Both wore dark suits
and hats that you could see had been tailored by
Tacey's expert hand, but these did not conceal a
certain defensive stiffness in the way they stood
there. Tacey looked controlled and dry-eyed but
Seely was crying bitterly. After the service Mr. and
Mrs. Herford came up and others, and by the time I
could get away, Tacey and Seely were gone.

When the long heavy dinner was over, Gaye took
me outside. He seemed to want to get away from
the house and all thoughts of the funeral. We
walked up the street together and I recall when I'd
seen Bisbee last it had been a blot of char and destruction. Today a brand-new Main Street stood
bright in the white Southwestern sunlight, shining
with fresh paint, spick and span with bricks not long
out of the kiln and still smelling, I thought, of lumber from the saw. Not a dark empty lot yawned on
Main Street and never a sign of blackened brick or
timber or the stink of burnt plaster. The Empire
Saloon stood in the same place, finer than ever. The
Waldorf restaurant might have never been destroyed except for a new, up-to-date sign with an
electric bulb hidden inside. The Maze, I noticed,

had a solid glass front now, and the City Barber Shop was new and shining from its bootblack chair to the fancy red and white awning out in front.

" The town's not doing so bad," Gaye agreed. " Why, we have twenty-six transfer wagons here now. Over a hundred and fifty telephones. I guess you didn't have time to see the new saloon in the gulch. It cashes four thousand in checks every payday. Plenty of money in the town. In fact, big plays on the tables don't go so strong any more. They have put in a brokers' ticker down in Brewery Gulch. Faro is going out. They're taking Wall Street fliers now."

We walked as far as Castle Rock.

" The Senator wants you to stay down here," Gaye mentioned as we turned around. " Just thought I'd tell you. He has a job for you."

" What doing? " I tried to be as casual and temperate as he.

" I don't know. But he'll put you up fast enough. He wants you around the house. He's getting old."

Just the way Gaye said: " He's getting old," and glanced to the right and left as if he had been made to feel for the first time that he was getting older himself, gave me a warmer feeling toward him. I knew that he would never say it, but something told me that he would like me to stay in Bisbee, too.

As we came back on the other side of the street, my eye fell on two windows above the Vienna bakery. One was lettered in gold: " MISS CROMWELL'S," and the next: " DRESSMAKING PARLORS." Down this far the buildings had not been burned, but this one had been refaced with the latest tapestry brick to keep in style with the new section. The front looked smart. The windows overlooked Main Street and had almost as good a location as the bank.

"Tacey must be doing pretty well," I said and looked the other way so I could not see Gaye's face.

"I think she is," he said calmly.

"Does she live up there? " I asked him.

I could feel his left eye, the sharper one, probing the side of my face.

"I understand she does."

"I want to go up and see her," I said.

"I think I'd wait a few days," he mentioned after a little.

"I want to see Seely before she goes," I said.

Gaye did not answer as we crossed the street. "Oh, hello, young feller! " he greeted William Williams, the old, rosy-cheeked, Cornish boss of the Czar shaft, who had squeezed his arm. In the post office he unlocked the bank box and glanced through the letters, opening and reading one or two type-written ones which he put in his pocket.

"Seely might not be going," he said to me as we went out.

"What do you mean? " I asked him.

"I don't know anything, Nugget." He met my glance squarely as he said it, and I knew that he told the truth. "Tacey's the one who got her here. She knew where she was. And you know Tacey."

"It's too late," I said bitterly.

"Maybe it is," he agreed, very quiet and firm. "But if anybody can do anything for that kid, it's Tacey."

We went slowly back to the house. As we opened the iron gate it seemed strange to have the thought come to me, but up on Youngblood Hill it had been Tacey and Seely and Gaye and I. Now here were the four of us again.